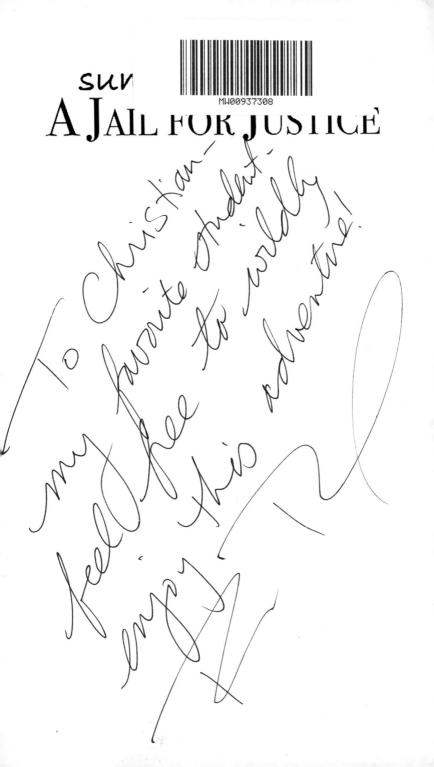

suv
A JAIL FOR JUSTICE

To Christian—
my favorite student—
feel free to wildly
enjoy this adventure!

summer island Books
by Robin Russell

A Prince in Peril

A Jail for Justice

A Karst in Kweilin *

* Forthcoming

summer island
A JAIL FOR JUSTICE

The character of Miss Fanny Pang was conceived by Lucy Michaels.

Summer Island—A Jail for Justice / by Robin Russell

Summary: When a group of children discover a mysterious box
they gain the clues to free a man unjustly imprisoned.

ISBN 978-0-9841884-1-3

Printed in USA
First Edition

To Mom, for lasting.

Acknowledgements

Hands down, Ngoc Do, editor and friend extraordinaire, is singularly responsible for the success of this book. Fearlessly and faithfully she ensured it would see the cloudless light of day. Thank you, Ngoc.

Running a close second would have to be Dennis Van Zandt, whose tireless and heartfelt nit-picking have made this book one of which even an English teacher can be proud.

My sincerest appreciation to Michelle Funk for her last-minute copy editing, loophole poking and ego bolstering.

As always, my undying gratitude to my family for their patience and my readers for their impatience.

Finally, specific thanks to my daughter, Giovanna, who implored me on a daily basis to write the next chapter and even when I had, begged me to read the first one over again.

❧ Contents ❦

summer island
A JAIL FOR JUSTICE

1

❧ The Box ❦

The man placed the last item in the box and sealed it, along with his own fate. It was done. Anxiously he checked the window, fearful that someone might have followed him. He had precious little time and still needed to decide on an address. The question plagued him: where to send it. There was no family left but was there a friend, a neighbor who could be trusted? It all needed to be done so delicately but he had too little time. It was strange, after all the weeks spent in meticulous planning, to be rushed at the last moment.

The man sighed.

The house will be empty of course but could it be addressed here even so? Sending it to the jail itself certainly wasn't an option. He looked at his watch—nearly half past five. There was no more time. It wasn't ideal but it would have to suffice. If Walt at the post office received an undeliverable package, perhaps he'd feel obligated to track down someone who'd know what to do with it—especially once he recognized the recipient's name.

Subconsciously the man began calculating the chances that the box would be sent as instructed, found and opened. Forty percent—maybe a little less. Factor in the chances of someone actually understanding what was in the box—that was a different story. *But what is there to do about that now?*

The address was written in his small leather notebook but he didn't need to check. He had it memorized. He'd known it before everything happened and afterward, everyone knew it. It had become *The House*. People in town, even as far away as Portland and Boston, had been talking about it. Murder. You never forget an address like that. He couldn't if he tried.

Quickly he scrawled it on the outside of the box. The boy would bring it to the post office and then it'd be their problem. He set the box on the counter. It weighed so little—barely a kilogram and yet it held a man's freedom inside. *How much should a man's freedom weigh?* he wondered. Even he couldn't begin to gauge that and immediately chastised himself for being so sentimental as to even think of such a thing anyway.

The man used his arm to sweep away the debris from the kitchen counter. He set the box in the middle—exactly where he told the boy it would be. He took a quarter out of his pocket and set it next to the box. He left no note. *Notes cause trouble and I've got enough of that as it is.* Besides, he wouldn't need one. The boy knew the instructions. Come to the house at six, side entrance. The kitchen door will be left open. Take the box on the counter and deliver it to the post office. The other half of the payment is next to it.

How much simpler could it be?

He grabbed his coat and his own small bag. He didn't need much. Everything he'd ever need, ever want, would be waiting for him once he got to New York City. The money was there—or at least his half. But it was more than enough. He'd already booked a room at the *Ritz-Carlton*—their best suite. Of course he couldn't use his real name anymore and that was a shame. All those years spent establishing a reputation for himself, earning the recognition, the glory and now it was gone. Still, you can't have it all. And a name, an identity, are small prices to pay for a lifetime of luxury.

Now there were only a few things separating him from that new life: a plane, two taxis and this box. As agreed, he left the door slightly ajar. He twisted the lock so all the boy would have to do is shut the door on his way out.

The man left The House.

And although the man had spent much time at The House there are just some things one doesn't know about a place unless one actually *lives* there. For example, he wouldn't necessarily know that the upstairs bathroom faucet would drip if the nozzle wasn't left a tad askew. Or that the third stair above the landing squeaked and should be avoided if you didn't want to wake the baby. And since he had never resided in The House, he did not know about the subtle slant in the kitchen floor—practically imperceptible. He did not know the way the window at the end of the hall would swell in warmer weather just enough so it could never quite close, leaving a tiny gap for air to get through. He certainly wouldn't know the way these two separate factors fit together so perfectly, lined up just so, that the cross breeze coming up from the ocean would draw air in such flawless alignment that the kitchen door could never stay open.

This didn't happen all at once. It was probably ten minutes after the man had left. Ten minutes of the door shifting slightly, to and fro, before—*slam*—it was closed. Locked.

This is how the boy found it twenty minutes later.

"What's wrong, Billy?" his friend asked, shifting a fishing pole to the other hand.

"The guy said the kitchen door would be open." The boy jiggled the handle but the door wouldn't budge.

"You think he was just joshin' you?"

"Nah, he was serious. Kinda' creepy too. But it's a quarter and that means a new fishing pole." Billy put his open palms on either side of his head to shield the sun. He pressed his face against the window.

"See anything?"

"I think I see the box. Boy, it's a mess in there." He turned to his friend. "Think we should break the window?"

"Are you mad? Crazy-lady Pang lives right next door. She'd be over here in a heartbeat."

"I suppose so." Billy hesitated, reluctant to give up the other half of his payment.

"Look, you still have the first quarter he gave you. I'll give you my old pole—it's not half bad, you know. You can save the money for something else."

"Yeah, you're right. Miss Pang would be over here in a stitch. She could hear an ant swallow."

"Attaboy. Now c'mon. This place is really giving me the willies. Say, check out those plants, huh?"

Billy looked to where his friend was pointing. It was odd. The owner of The House had planted flowers willy-nilly around the yard.

"Yeah, pretty strange."

"I'll say."

The boys set out for the stream, their minds filled with images of catching fish and maybe even camping out if their mothers would let them. And as time passed, they forgot about The House and the box and the strange man and the locked door. And eventually, even the quarter.

As anyone who has ever tended plants will tell you, a summer garden will take over if you don't keep an eye on it. And since there was no one to keep an eye on it—not even Miss Fanny Pang, who was so disgusted with it she closed her kitchen shade to banish it from sight—that is exactly what happened to this garden. The wisteria, which had been planted so liberally the summer before because his daughter had liked the smell of it, crept upward, ensnaring the gutters and chimney. The rhododendrons, with their brash bouquets, seemed to double in size as June turned to July and July to August. And so on with the clematis, the lavender and the hydrangeas. Even the comically-planted flowers on the large unkempt lawn—looking like some 50-foot-tall housewife had dropped a bag of groceries and scattered the contents higgledy-piggledy across the parking lot of the local Shop 'n' Save—grew and spread and grew and spread.

By late October all of the flowers and deciduous greenery were gone, replaced with the shocking reds and oranges of autumn in New England. Then winter, when everything looked dead but wasn't in the least. So that by the time spring came and the first crocuses poked their heads through the disarrayed mayhem, the vegetation had expanded to such a degree that even the one who planted it would not have recognized it. The infusion of sunlight and warmth and water brought life back to the garden, which had now become an entity in and of itself—a wild animal with no one brave enough to tame it.

And so it went on like this. Miss Fanny Pang muttering oaths under her breath as she gradually drew every north-facing shade in her house, in an annual attempt to cast out the eyesore. Every year she'd complain to the town selectman but he'd say there was nothing he could do. After all, it was The House.

Finally enough years passed for the small house to be fully consumed by the garden. At this point, Miss Fanny Pang convinced herself it was no longer her neighbor's outrageous landscaping but the forest itself that abutted her property. One by one, she re-opened the shades, which allowed her to enjoy her forest view along with the view of the ocean and her lawn and the seldom-traveled Old Mill Road leading into town.

Within Miss Fanny Pang's forest—which is how others had come to think of it as well—The House was alive with activity. Boards were rotting through. Pipes, which had frozen in winter from lack of use, had burst and water flooded the entire downstairs. Wallpaper—periwinkle to match the wisteria—peeled away. Snow on the roof, left unshoveled, accumulated throughout the winter, gradually weighing down so heavily that it collapsed into the attic—letting in more water and more wisteria. Dust collected on the dishes—two cups, two bowls and two spoons—which had been left to dry on a red and white checkered towel next to the sink.

In fact, the box itself, which sat unmoved on the counter, was probably the only thing in that house or in the surrounding environs, which was never altered in any way. So year after year after year, until an entire decade had passed, it rested, undelivered and hidden from the world.

2

❧ The Arrival ❧

Greta Washington was riding in a twin-engine wobbly jalopy of a plane and she wasn't the least bit scared. After what she had been through the previous summer, there was precious little that could cause anything remotely close to fear in this twelve-year-old. Well, unless of course it was water, but she was working on that. It was one of her many self-improvement projects. Greta was designing herself into the perfect human being. Perfect for her anyway. Greta would be the first to admit that perfection, like most attributes, was subjective.

Subjective, Greta thought to herself as the plane skipped along air currents in its journey to The Island. *What a wonderful word.* Greta's appreciation (some might call it an obsession) with words was one of the things she was planning to keep from the O.G.D. (Old Greta Days). She loved language—loved how it could playfully twist and turn one thing into another. It was fluid. It was coercive. It was grand.

At this moment however, Greta's giddiness had nothing at all to do with language. It had been nearly ten months since she'd been to Deer Isle, Maine—where she would spend the entire summer—and she could barely contain her excitement. Last year had been her first visit, which made her the youngest of the five children who would be staying at Tia's mansion for the holiday.

She could still vividly remember that bewildered thrill—exactly one year ago—when she returned home to find a mysterious envelope and a mother who was uncharacteristically jubilant. The invitation—lavender in both color and scent—was just a few sentences long. However, the plane ticket inside told plenty. It was an opportunity for frolic and splendor beyond even her impressive imagination. Of course, the fact that she wouldn't have to spend her summer at the Trenton Children's Center (which Greta secretly referred to as "Poor Camp") was responsible for much of her happiness.

This year's invitation had also arrived just a few days before she needed to leave, but this time she was much more prepared. She knew why she only needed to bring a few things. The girls' room had a small department store shoved into one giant closet. She knew when her plane landed at *Logan Airport*, she would not be met by an adult, but by a girl only a year older, who would hire a local pilot to fly them the rest of the way. Greta knew Tia's prize-winning food would be within arm's reach on an hourly basis, unlike Tia herself, who would inevitably be occupied with a variety of projects, leaving her underage guests to amuse and fend for themselves. Most importantly, Greta knew she'd be spending the next ten weeks with four of the most wonderful people in the entire world.

She smiled uncontrollably, not even considering for a moment that two of those very people, who were crammed into the plane with her right now, might think her foolish. Gazing down at the shrinking cars and houses, Greta felt as if even she could unfold wings and soar to The Island like an eagle. Summer vacation had begun.

Impulsively she turned to her companion, a plump girl with curly black hair and eyes to match. Dinora had flown in from Mexico City that morning, as she had for the past three summers. This time though, she traveled alone. Her brother, Mario, who had accompanied her on every other visit, was now studying at MIT in Boston. He had secured an internship with *Haverhill Chemicals*, a prestigious pharmaceutical company and would be too busy this year to join them.

One might have thought that Dinora would be afraid to travel so far by herself. If so, that person could not have been more mistaken. Dinora's moxie was one of the many characteristics Greta admired in her friend and she had included it (along with learning Spanish) in her plan. *I'll be plucky like Dinora*, Greta had told herself. *I'll have moxie!*

As with any friend, there were also things which Greta didn't care to emulate.

"It's so bumpy. Greta, don't you think it's bumpy? Has it always been this bumpy? Excuse me, pilot person? Is it supposed to be this bumpy? I don't remember it being this bumpy last time."

And that would be it, Greta continued her private musings. Although Dinora's constant prattling and scatterbrained ramblings were an endearing trait, they certainly weren't ones Greta had any interest in copying. She considered this a moment. *She* found them endearing but they drove Zoë mad. And if Zoë were here right now, Dinora would not be going on this long. It was almost as if that's how Dinora knew to stop—when Zoë snapped or glared at her.

Zoë was another story. To this day, Greta had never met anyone braver. The girl knew no fear and somehow seemed assured that no matter what she did, everything would turn out well for her. This included crash-landing a plane, jumping off a cliff, facing down a man with a gun and taking on the town bully. But all of this paled in comparison to what Zoë had done for Greta last summer. She had saved her life. Technically she had let her drown (hence the fear of water) and *then* saved her life, but Greta tried not to get too hung up on technicalities. *And I'll be brave, like Zoë,* she instructed herself.

After Greta had recovered from nearly drowning, Zoë started taking her to the Lily Pond near Tia's house, where she taught her to swim. Over the remaining weeks of their summer break, Greta had learned the basics. During the school year, she and her mother had taken lessons at their local YMCA. She wasn't great but she could swim and she wasn't afraid. *I am not afraid. I am not afraid,* Greta repeated in a silent mixture of confirmation and hope. In truth, she was petrified. Not of swimming necessarily but of the ocean itself. Even last year, when she and her friends had gone to their secret cove, Greta tried to go in the water. The scent of the sea rekindled her memory and she had nearly fainted. She knew this was all in her head and planned to take one step farther into the ocean each day until she had no choice but to swim in it. This, above everything else from the O.G.D., was the thing of which Greta most wanted to rid herself. She punctuated this thought with a sharp, succinct nod.

"I wonder what happened to Zoë," Dinora began a new stream of questioning. "Why wasn't she on the flight? Seymour, are you certain you didn't hear anything?"

The tall blonde boy in the front seat turned around. "I'm positive, Dinora," he answered fretfully. "I'm just as much at a loss as you."

Greta wasn't surprised to see him worried. Seymour was that kind of person. He was only fifteen but he looked and acted much older. The first was due to his size. Seymour was enormous—as large as Greta was small. When the five of them were together, she had to stand far enough away so her neck wouldn't get a crick as she craned to see him. He was taller than most grown men. He was broad-shouldered but soft-spoken and Greta thought of him as a gentle giant. In a fairy tale, he'd be the one terrorizing the town until the citizens would realize they'd misunderstood and that he'd actually been protecting them all along. This was the second part. Seymour protected everyone. Helpless animals, old people, lost children. Everyone. Including his cousin, Zoë, to her endless annoyance. To be honest though, Zoë did get annoyed quite easily and, along with Dinora's chattiness, this was a trait Greta didn't plan to take on.

Seymour wasn't the only one worried. Greta too thought it strange that Zoë hadn't been on the plane from Shanghai. Of the five children, the two cousins were the only ones actually related to Tia, who was their grandmother's younger sister. They'd been spending their summers on The Island ever since they were babies. Every summer for fifteen years. So where was she this year? And why?

Greta knew that Zoë's other grandmother, who took care of her during her parents' frequent travels, didn't approve of her spending summers on The Island. Zoë never spoke about her life in China, but from what Greta could gather, it was exceedingly—she searched her mind for the right word—*proper*. Greta could easily imagine Zoë's response to that assessment: a resounding and sarcastic "Hah!" most likely, or "That's an understatement."

Life on The Island was anything but proper. Except for a handful of Tia's expectations, the children were allowed full rein for the summer. Greta was sure Mrs. Chen found that disgusting, disreputable and despicable. Zoë, on the other hand, found it liberating. Thus it became one of the many issues over which they argued, although Greta pictured any arguments between them probably boiled down to one woman yelling and one girl grumbling. In fact, her grandmother had become so disposed against the idea of Zoë's annual escapades that she had refused to pay for the trip. This spurred an entirely new drama when Zoë, who was startlingly beautiful—until she opened her mouth and yelled at you—agreed to do some modeling work in order to pay for the trip. She loathed it, Greta knew, but that was the deal.

"We're landing!" Dinora squealed. "Finally, we're here! We're here! Oh, Greta, aren't you thrilled? Aren't you simply thrilled? I'm so thrilled. Seymour, are you—"

"I'm thrilled, Dinora." Even his anxiety couldn't keep Seymour from laughing.

The plane teetered as it slowly settled onto the tarmac. And who should be there to greet them?

"Zoë!" Dinora cried, hurling herself out of her seat before being snatched back by the seatbelt she'd forgotten to unfasten. Greta stayed where she was. She knew better than to be in Dinora's way. The girl was exceedingly fast and determined.

"Hello, Dinora," Zoë said calmly, preparing herself for the verbal onslaught.

But even Dinora didn't have a chance. Before she could open her mouth, Seymour had stormed over to Zoë and begun shouting at her in Mandarin.

Greta didn't understand any of the words but the sentiment was loud and clear. He hated it when Zoë veered from the agreed-upon plan. He said it was selfish and infuriating but everyone knew, except somehow Zoë herself, that he really meant it terrified him. *Fear can certainly look a lot like anger*, thought Greta, as she watched the two cousins.

"So I came early," Zoë said, casually shifting to the language where Seymour was bound to show more restraint.

"Would it have killed you to tell someone? We waited forever for your flight!"

"It was . . . unexpected. Anyway, we're all here now so why worry about it? Hi, Greta!"

"Hi." Greta didn't know quite what to do with herself. She felt like she should give Zoë a hug or something. They'd grown so close last summer. But Zoë wasn't exactly the hugging type.

Zoë gave her a quizzical expression before shrugging her shoulders. "Okay, truck's here—let's go."

"Is that Danny?" Dinora shouted, running toward the old pickup truck heading their direction. It screeched to a halt, barely missing the madly-waving girl, who didn't seem to notice. "Danny, you're driving!"

The boy smiled. "I just got my permit. I'm supposed to have an adult with me but Edith said it was okay as long I stay on The Island."

"Wow," sighed an awestruck Dinora. "Driving."

Greta could tell Dinora was dreaming of what that would be like.

But Dinora, being a girl of action, didn't dream long. "Let me try." She swung open the driver's side door and started to get in.

"No!" four voices blurted in unison. Seymour guided Dinora away from the door and helped her into the back. He gave Greta a hand up before climbing in himself. Zoë joined Daniel in the cab, laughing at the remnants of his panic.

Within seconds, they were on their way.

This was Greta's favorite part. It had only happened once before but it already felt like a ritual. The truck wended its way along the coastline, gradually approaching Tia's incredible home. Greta took stock of the cliffs, the dense forest and the sunset painting the ocean's surface in gold. Tia didn't like them arriving after dark and they had made it just in time.

The road turned and there, backed by a bronze cliff, was a house so large that Greta, who had lived there for an entire summer, had only been in half the rooms. It still took her breath away. The road turned again and the house was out of sight. A silence came over the children. It had been like this last year too, almost in sacred preparation for their summer. Then the house was back in view, even more majestic in every detail. Greta saw the surroundings were just as they had left them: the enormous garden, a large barn, an orchard farther out and the surrounding fields dipping on one side into a bluff which surveyed the ocean. On the other side, the fields met a wood which had once hidden their escape. It all seemed so long ago.

And although this was her favorite part, the *best* part was going to be the warm, melodic voice of Tia. But when they arrived, Tia was not standing outside, as usual. *That's not exactly accurate*, Greta corrected herself. She'd only been here once before. Just because Tia had been outside to welcome them last year didn't mean it was her regular habit. But the others too seemed surprised at Tia's absence. Seymour and Dinora looked at each other and shrugged simultaneously.

Daniel braked a little too quickly and the truck lurched to a stop. Within seconds, the children had grabbed their few belongings and bounded into the large kitchen, where they found a note:

My Darlings,

I'm terribly sorry not to be here to greet you myself. Edith and I have been called away and must attend to some matters on the mainland. There is stew on the stove. I left bread and a pie in the pantry.

I look forward to seeing each of you.

All my love and welcome back to The Island, Tia

"Did she say what kind of pie? I've been dying to have some of her strawberry rhubarb but the apple is divine and—"

Seymour interrupted Dinora and pointed to the note where Tia had written,

P.S. Blueberry

"Oh, my favorite!" Dinora exclaimed.

"Daniel, did Tia say anything to you?" asked Seymour.

"Not a word. She was here when we left. They must have just gone."

"But the note doesn't seem rushed." Seymour began to chew absentmindedly on his lower lip—a sure sign he was trying to puzzle out something.

"It's nothing," Zoë said, a little too quickly. "We should eat."

"Let's wash up first," said Dinora. "Then we can have dinner at seven sharp."

They all laughed at this and Dinora beamed. There wasn't a single clock in Tia's home. Still, she served dinner nightly at "seven sharp", which in Tia's mind directly coincided with when dinner happened to be ready.

Seymour and Daniel ascended the back stairs, which led from the kitchen to the boys' room, where Seymour would be staying. Daniel, who had lived with Tia for the past four years, had his own bedroom on the third floor. The girls moved through the large dining and living rooms, past the parlor and music room to the front stairs, which led to the girls' room.

As they entered they were immersed in memories. No girl said anything as she recalled the previous summer's adventures. Their friend Peter had gone into hiding after his parents—the king and queen of Lesotho—had been killed in a military coup d'état. Now he was living in exile and no one knew where.

"It gets so I don't even want to watch the news anymore," Dinora said. "And now the influenza. It just seems like more and more people are dying every day. One of the boys in fourth grade lost his father to it. Sometimes I feel as if the whole world were falling apart."

"Probably because it pretty much is," said Zoë.

"And then I think of how far we've come and what we've been able to accomplish over the years. I know that someday—"

"Your prince will come?" Zoë warbled, swooning dramatically before collapsing on the rose-printed sofa.

"You just wait, Zoë Chen," Dinora pouted. "One of these days—"

"Oh relax, Dinora. You're so sensitive. Can't you even take a joke?"

"Is that what it was supposed to be?"

Greta slipped quietly out of the room, although she probably could have stormed out screaming and the two girls wouldn't have noticed. Zoë and Dinora were very different from each other and except for the occasional derisive comment (usually from Zoë) they found a way to get along. *I hope the whole summer isn't going to be like this*, Greta thought. She'd had enough adventure and discord the previous year to last a lifetime and she was eagerly awaiting a perfectly boring and delicious summer holiday.

As she was mulling this over, she was gravitating toward Tia's library. It was by far Greta's most treasured room. Centered on the second floor, its vaulted ceiling topped a perfectly circular room, three-quarters of which was covered in floor-to-ceiling, built-in bookcases. The wall was completed with a massive span of glass overlooking the Atlantic Ocean. The room itself was filled with overstuffed furniture, tables and lamps. A hearth was cut out of one section of the wall and boasted a large fireplace. It was too warm for a fire tonight but summer evenings on The Island would get cold enough.

The feature which most delighted Greta, however, was the ladder attached at the top to a metal track running along the ceiling. She climbed it now, not bothering to roll it to a specific place. There was no orderly arrangement of the books. One could find a two-hundred-year-old diary next to a fashion magazine from last week's newsstand. It was a librarian's nightmare. Greta adored the quirkiness of the arrangement. It was like the room itself was throwing up its arms, saying, "Eh, what can you do?"

She pulled out a book halfway up and climbed the remaining rungs to perch happily on the top step—her very own crow's nest. She opened the book and discovered, to her amusement, that it was a yearbook from *Deer Isle High School*, Class of 1922. Greta firmly believed there was something of value in every book. She turned to the first page of this one and settled down to find it.

It didn't take very long to finish. As Greta replaced the book on the shelf, another one—faded brown with the title embossed in gold—caught her eye. It was called *Up from Slavery* and when she opened it she was surprised to see it autographed by the author himself. He'd written, "To Dorothea, I'm expecting great things from you. Booker T. Washington." She pondered this for a moment and began to consider something exciting but improbable. After all, it was a common enough surname.

"Greta?"

She squeaked as Daniel's voice startled her. She hadn't realized how much time had passed.

He smiled and said, "It's seven."

3

✺ The Prudence ✺

Greta awoke to sunshine, sea air and the sounds of joyful conversations below. Her first morning back on The Island!

She quickly chose clothes from the gigantic closet supplied with anything a girl might need for the summer. She dashed downstairs, hearing a welcome and familiar voice.

"Tia!" she cried, running toward the woman she had dearly missed, embracing her and not letting go.

"There, there, Greta. It's not as if I'd moved out, dear," she laughed easily.

"Where were you? Is everything all right?" Greta asked.

"Don't you mind about that. It's all taken care of now and there are better things to think about. Much better things." Tia motioned to the large dining room table. "Breakfast, for instance. Come, my darlings. Sit and eat. Sit and eat. It won't get any hotter."

The children did not have to be told twice. The meal displayed before them was heaven sent. There was real clotted cream, fresh raspberries, quiche and Tia's famous beignets. An urn on the buffet contained steaming hot chocolate and a small carafe produced the rich scent of coffee. Seymour reached for some before piling food onto his plate. Greta hadn't noticed any of this the night before and presumed Tia must have been cooking for hours this morning. She turned to thank her but her host had vanished back into the kitchen.

Greta had taken a large bite of a homemade donut, which had been tossed in powdered sugar, when Zoë pounded her fist on the table, declaring, "I want to go sailing and I want you all to come with me." She turned toward Greta and softened her tone considerably. "Even you."

Greta's throat seized at the thought. Unfortunately, she was in mid-swallow. She began to choke violently and crumbs of half-chewed donut splattered into the air.

"I know the Heimlich Maneuver!" Dinora shouted, thrusting her hand into the air as if shouting out the correct answer in class. "I *do*! My teacher taught us in Biology. Well, not in Biology *exactly*. Technically, we were in the hallway outside the classroom. You see, Dulce Maria was chewing on some *chicle* and I asked her—"

"Oh shut up, Dinora!" Zoë snapped, instantly drawing everyone's attention. They all knew she got annoyed with the garrulous girl easily but she'd never yelled at her like this. Even Greta was so surprised that she swallowed the donut bite whole.

"Hot chocolate, please." Her voice was weak but sounded much louder in the complete quiet of the dining room.

"Here, Greta," said Zoë, quickly pouring a cup, cooling it down with extra cream and passing it to her. Greta accepted it appreciatively and took a long drink. The warm liquid helped dissolve the food and she began to catch her breath.

When she was finally breathing normally again, she said, "I think I'm done eating for now."

The subsequent laughter jumpstarted the breakfast and soon everything was back to normal. Greta loved this part—the multi-layered conversations, the clutter of food and dishes. She lived alone with her mother and it was always so calm. Either one of them was talking, or the other, or neither. Having four other people and five other conversations was a treat for her. It was impossible to feel lonely.

"Well?" Seymour asked when they had finished breakfast and begun clearing the dishes. "Shall we hike up to Star Rock or ride the horses? We could head into town or swim in the Lily Pond." He made a point of looking at every face except the one belonging to his cousin. His gaze rested on Dinora's expectantly.

"If you want my opinion," she paused to confirm this with Seymour, who nodded obligingly. "Well, I personally think that nothing in this world, nay this entire galaxy, would be more wonderful and splendid and fun and good and fine than . . . than—oh, I forgot what I was going to say."

Greta could hear Zoë's jaw clench.

"Oh right, now I remember. I think we should go sailing!" she announced delightedly.

Zoë's relief was obvious. "Thank you, Dinora."

"Oh, don't thank me yet! Truth is, I don't know the first thing about sailing. Someone will have to teach me so I don't wreck the boat. Oh! Sorry, Zoë." Dinora said contritely.

Zoë took a visibly deep breath. "Don't mention it," she said and it was clear she meant exactly that.

"Of course. I figured you might be sensitive about wrecking Tia's boat because at the time, she really seemed upset. I think I even remember her saying something about—"

"Like I said, Dinora. Don't—mention—it."

"Mention what, dear?" Tia asked, reentering the room.

"Nothing, Tia," said Zoë.

"Tia, we were thinking about going sailing today. That is if you don't need us for something," said Seymour.

"Sailing? Oh, that does sound lovely. Quite lovely." She seemed distracted as she sorted through some papers in the small secretary at one end of the room. Then she stopped, turned and looked Zoë squarely in the face.

"Sailing," she repeated, arching one eyebrow.

"I'll be more careful. Man, can't a girl make a mistake these days?"

"Darling, you ruined my boat."

Zoë opened her mouth to respond but seemed to think better of it, unsure of what she could possibly say in her defense.

Tia nodded knowingly. "Daniel, will you go with them?"

"I'd like to—as long as you or Edith don't need me." The excitement was clear in his voice.

"Oh, I can't think of a place I need you *more* than with my niece on *The Prudence*. Not one place indeed."

"*The Prudence?*" Seymour asked.

"Yes. *The Prudence.*" Tia emphasized the new name. "Originally it was called *The Defender II*," Tia explained to Greta. "After the boat my father sailed to win the America's Cup in 1895, but after Zoë's mishap, I realized that Zoë was the one from whom she'd need to defend herself. So I named her *The Prudence*, hoping my niece would show some."

"Oh," Zoë said.

Tia seemed to consider all of this. "Very well, you may go but Daniel is in charge. You understand, Zoë? My great uncle was one of the finest lobstermen The Island has ever seen. He left me that sloop and it holds a great deal of sentimental value for me. A great deal. *Daniel* is in charge."

"Got it!" Zoë looked as if she would have agreed to anything at this point—she was just so happy to go.

Quickly the children worked together to clean up the breakfast dishes and pack for the day. As was typical, Greta found herself preparing their lunch with Seymour. They packed the meal as Zoë issued instructions to the rest.

"Dinora—sunglasses and hats for everyone. Daniel—get the truck ready. If we drive down to the harbor we'll cut at least a half hour off the trip, leaving more time to be on the boat. Seymour—lunch. Greta—"

"Fascinating, Daniel," Seymour teased. "What a unique approach to being in charge."

"Yes," Daniel laughed and put his arm around Zoë's shoulders. "It's very modern. It's called delegation."

"Hey," Zoë said. "She said *on* the boat, you know. We're not even out of the house yet."

"Okay, skipper. You're in charge," Seymour called out. "Oh wait, no you're—"

"Seymour, don't mess with me. Not today." There was an edge in her voice and since all of the children had experienced Zoë's temper on numerous occasions, they each saw the benefit of giving her some slack.

"Okay, okay. Greta and I will pack the lunch."

This seemed to satisfy Zoë and the next hour went smoothly. The drive down to the harbor seemed to take forever, as all of the children were getting excited about being on the boat. All except Greta. She hadn't said a word since breakfast. It was all she could do not to faint entirely. *I can swim. I can swim. I can swim.* She repeated her mantra so rapidly to herself that the words morphed together until they didn't even make sense any longer.

"Greta?" It was Seymour's voice. She opened her eyes, not realizing they had been closed. "We're here."

She looked around. The others had already left the truck and were making their way down the wharf to where the boat was moored.

"Seymour?"

"I know, Greta. You don't have to go if you don't want."

Greta thought about this. Last summer had been the same, at the beginning. The others wanted to explore a mysterious (and quite possibly dangerous) cave. Even the thought of this had frightened her. She had lectured herself then and tried to recall those words now. They helped a little but what finally made the difference was remembering her self-improvement plan. Not sailing with her friends was definitely something from the O.G.D. and she'd do well to be rid of it.

"I'll try," she said, with manufactured confidence.

"Then let's go." Seymour opened the passenger side door and helped her out. When they joined the others at the boat, Zoë was already aboard and well into her instructions.

"—and this here's the bow pulpit. There's the anchor, that's the boom—be careful of that—and here's the winch to hoist the mainsail." She surveyed the boat, nodding as it met with her satisfaction. Her hands were on her hips and one foot was resting on the starboard edge. With her hair pulled back, sunglasses and a faded captain's hat, she cut quite a figure.

"So which end is the front?" Dinora asked, squinting to look up at their *de facto* leader.

Zoë stared back at her with an expression of utter disdain. "Dinora, if you don't pay attention, you can hardly expect—"

"Why don't we start from the beginning again?" Daniel said, helping Dinora onto the boat. He turned to offer his hand to Greta.

She had fainted.

"Oh, for goodness' sake," groaned Zoë. "At this rate, we'll never leave. Here, let me get her." Zoë leapt gracefully off the boat and made her way to the girl. Greta would have been small for a ten-year-old, let alone twelve. Zoë picked her up easily and slung her gently over her shoulder. She passed Greta's limp body to Seymour who had also boarded. Daniel was now at the helm. He'd started the motor and was shifting the boat into reverse. The sound was music to Zoë's ears and a look of sheer relief, gratitude and joy came across her face. She hurriedly untied the ropes, pushed the boat away from the dock and leapt back on. Her priorities were clear. She went to Greta first, whom Seymour had laid below deck and who was just coming back to consciousness.

"I'll help Daniel," said Seymour, leaving the cramped underbelly of the boat. Zoë nodded toward him distractedly as she helped Greta sit up.

"Are we," the younger girl began hesitantly.

"Greta, I'm not going to mince words. We're on the boat and we're going sailing. You're just going to have to cope. Can you do that?"

"I can try," she smiled wanly.

"Greta, what's the worst possible scenario?"

"I could drown."

"Exactly. And that's already happened. And you survived." Zoë hunkered down next to her. "Look, you are just going to have to decide what kind of person you want to be in this world. Are you just going to let one bad experience ruin a lifetime of fun? Are you going to let people run your life for you or are you going to take charge and do what you want to do? Sometimes you just need to take matters into your own hands."

Greta was getting the distinct feeling that Zoë wasn't necessarily talking about a fear of water at this point but about her own situation. *Even so*, Greta thought. *It is true*. So what if she had planned to reintroduce herself to the Atlantic Ocean with the one-step-farther-each-day handshake. That time had passed. Now she was smack in the middle and over her head. Literally.

With Zoë leading the way, the two girls emerged from the hull. Greta opened one eye, then the other. The view was breathtaking. The sun was nearing its apex and there was nothing but blue sky above them. The wind was strong but the boat still held steady.

"Just wait until the sail is up," Zoë whispered, motioning for Greta to sit on the portside bench. Seymour and Dinora were on the other end with Daniel, who was giving them an introductory sailing lesson at a rate they could actually comprehend.

He looked up at Zoë, smiling. "I thought you'd appreciate getting out on the open seas."

Zoë nodded vigorously and started to speak. But before she could, Daniel cut her off.

"We're here but we can't raise the mainsail until everyone knows the basics of boat safety."

"Fair enough," Zoë said, grudgingly. "So here are the life jackets." She reached underneath the bench to open a small cabinet. She tossed one to Greta (who looked exceptionally relieved) before donning one herself. "And keep your fingers away from the lines." She looked at Daniel. "Let's go."

"There's actually a little more to it than that," he said, trying not to laugh.

"Somehow I expected as much," added Seymour, teasing his cousin playfully with one glance.

Zoë was beginning to look like a wild animal, pacing in her cage.

Daniel sighed sympathetically. "But I suppose it's enough to at least get started. Seymour and Dinora, come over here and hold the helm. Zoë and I will show you how to use the halyard to hoist the mainsail." He grinned at her. "Then we can really fly." He turned to face the tiny shivering girl clutching her already-secured life vest. "Greta, you're doing great. Just stay where you are."

Greta looked as if she couldn't possibly do anything but that, even if she wanted. She tried to be brave and at least look at the water. To her surprise, it had a soothing effect, especially focusing on the horizon, which skimmed the vastness of the ocean. She turned and saw Daniel and Zoë working together to crank what looked to her to be the metal top of an over-sized pepper mill. Slowly, the white sail crept upward, catching the wind and whipping back and forth. The boat began to pull in response and the large perpendicular pole (before she fainted, Greta thought she remembered it being called a "boom") was struggling to break free.

"You have to be careful here," explained Daniel. "Make sure the boom is directly facing the wind. Otherwise it could tip the boat or rip the sail."

The huge sheet of white fabric made its final surge and Daniel tied it off before reclaiming the helm, politely declining Zoë's offer to help steer. He turned the boat to harness the wind and instantly they were soaring so quickly that The Island was soon out of sight.

For a long time each of the children was silent. Zoë, now that they were fully at sea, seemed lost in her own world as she checked lines and eventually, under Daniel's close supervision, took the helm. Seymour, Greta and, surprisingly, Dinora too were speechless as they traversed farther along the ocean's surface. It was hypnotizing. Daniel, who occasionally gave instructions or explanations, provided the only human sound.

Finally, as all had been expecting to happen far sooner, Dinora broke the spell. "Shall we eat?" she asked excitedly, making her way to where they had stored the picnic basket. Reluctantly at first, the children let their attention be called away from the water. But after the first whiff of food, their hunger rushed forward and each was more than delighted to devour the delicious meal they had packed.

All in all, it was a most invigorating day and even Greta was disappointed to see it end so soon, although she was certainly more eager than the rest, by far.

This time when the truck rumbled along the driveway Tia was waiting for them. But it was certainly not with open arms. Greta had seen Tia happy and content. She'd seen her worried and even scared. She had never once seen her cross but at this moment Tia must have been livid. She glared at them as she waited for Daniel to cut the engine.

The children got out of the truck and inched toward her, each clueless of what to expect. They didn't have to wait long.

"Zoë Qingyue Contrara Chen," Tia began, in an ice-cold voice. "You march upstairs right now and pack your bag. You are going home."

4

❧ The Address ❧

If it hadn't been for Seymour the others wouldn't have had any idea about what took place in the few hours that followed. While they had been shocked by Tia's tone and her orders, Zoë hadn't looked surprised in the least. But soon the children were separated as Tia stormed into the kitchen with Zoë closely at her heels, imploring her to hear reason.

The others passed the time by unpacking and waiting. They were certain when they finished they would have some inkling as to what was going on. But half an hour later they still didn't know.

"We might as well wash up," suggested Dinora. "I highly doubt either of them will tell us what's happening anytime soon. We're just going to have to wait." As the others considered this, Dinora got a faraway look in her eyes. "Jasmine, I think." None of them needed to ask. Dinora was a connoisseur of scents and flavors in every form. She had plans for a bath. And although none of the others could imagine doing anything while something of such great importance lay in the balance, the idea of being clean and warm quickly appealed to them as well.

When there was still no sign, even after their baths, the children gathered in the large kitchen. The fact that Tia hadn't made dinner reinforced both the gravity of the situation and how long she must have been waiting for them to return. They found some leftovers in the pantry and pieced together a meager meal. This was just as well since, although they were famished from the day at sea, their stomachs were already half full with worry.

The ring of the telephone jarred against the quiet.

They looked at each other, wondering who would answer it. Seymour rose and walked toward the phone with a reverence one might reserve for a meeting with the Dalai Lama. He picked up the receiver just as Zoë and Tia entered the kitchen. The others sat in frozen observation.

"Uh, Witherspoon residence," he began. His face indicated a combination of surprise and concern. Greta couldn't understand what he said next. It was in Mandarin. As he spoke, a look of dread came over Zoë's countenance, which, up until now, had been layered in tears and stoic resolve. Seymour stretched the cord of the old-fashioned handset in Zoë's direction. "It's for you."

Zoë turned to Tia and seemed to communicate a silent question or plea. Tia nodded her response and Zoë stepped forward to the phone. "*Wei*?"

The voice that responded could have been heard on the neighboring island. Zoë winced and instinctually pulled the receiver away. Heard but not understood. The woman on the other end was speaking a dialect which even Seymour (who could hear clearly enough) was struggling to decipher. Only Tia seemed to have a crystal clear understanding of the conversation and the situation.

"*Nai Nai*—" Zoë began, before being cut off by the speaker, who apparently had bottomless lungs. Zoë tried the same sentence a few more times before giving up entirely and resorting to what Greta assumed to be the

Mandarin equivalent of "Yes, ma'am" for the next fifteen minutes.

Eventually, the voice stopped and Zoë turned to Tia. "They want to talk to you."

Before Tia took the phone she motioned for all of the children to leave the room. Seymour, who seemed to have gleaned some of what had taken place, was the most reluctant. Zoë's willingness was obvious as she darted out of the kitchen at the first indication of dismissal.

The others followed. Tia must have sensed when they were out of earshot because they didn't hear anything more. They found Zoë in the girls' room. She was sitting on one of the large armchairs, her knees pulled up to her chest and her arms wrapped around her legs.

"I know my *Hechihua* is a little rusty, so correct me if I'm wrong but am I to believe that you actually—"

"Please, Seymour. Not anymore. Not tonight." Zoë looked exhausted.

"Zoë, you can't just do something like this. Your grandmother—"

"You think I don't know that? Huh? You think I'm on some other planet. I knew exactly what she would do. I know better than you, *Ximei*!" she spat, her use of Seymour's childhood nickname revealing just how tired and sad and scared she must be. Greta went to her, climbing on the edge of the chair and opening her arms for the older girl to lean in. She held Zoë for a long time.

"Zo—" Seymour didn't know how to finish the sentence, but it was clear that his ire had dwindled to sympathy.

"Listen, we should probably all just try to get some sleep," Daniel suggested. "We have market tomorrow and my guess is that Zoë's had enough excitement for at least one day." He smiled at her and opened the door for Seymour, who didn't look any more eager to leave this room than he had the last one, but went with Daniel nonetheless.

Greta guided Zoë to the bathroom where she helped her wash up and get ready for bed. After tucking her in, Greta got ready herself. As she crawled underneath her down comforter, music began rising from beneath the floorboards.

Greta had wondered if this would happen. Every night Tia played the grand piano in the music room, which was directly below theirs. The boys' room was far bigger and included a breathtaking view but Zoë insisted the girls' room was better. Greta agreed. There was nothing quite like drifting off to sleep with beautiful sounds to pave the way. What made the arrangement even more special was that Tia used the songs to communicate with them. Usually the messages were so complicated that only Zoë, an exceptionally gifted student of music, could decipher them. It was probably true in this case as well but tonight Tia's mournful, somber music played to deaf ears. Zoë had fallen asleep as soon as her head met the pillow.

The day was cloudy when Greta woke and she felt the heaviness of the weather reflected in her own heart. As usual, she was the last one up and as she made her way downstairs her worried mind longed for one thing. She needed to hear Dinora's voice. Somehow, the incessant and optimistic chatter of her friend served as a barometer—signaling whether or not all was well with their world.

When Greta entered the dining room she found Dinora, completely silent and eating corn flakes. *This is surreal*, Greta thought to herself. She didn't even know Tia had cold cereal. She didn't even know it was possible for Dinora to be quiet—particularly first thing in the morning when she was usually her most ebullient.

Dinora passed Greta a bowl and the box of cereal. "The others are loading the truck," she said, dejectedly, looking utterly lost from the strange events of the night before.

Greta had no appetite but waited politely with her friend. As Dinora washed her bowl, Greta removed their errand list from its magnet on Tia's refrigerator. They joined the others, who were in an equally miserable mood, and made their way to the farmers market.

By the time they finished setting up their stall, the sun had fully risen. Now it began to peek through the clouds and warm the people below.

"She's letting me stay," Zoë cut to the chase. There was something in her tenor that Greta couldn't quite place but it certainly wasn't happiness.

"That's wonderful!" Dinora blurted. "Isn't that wonderful?" She beamed at the others.

No one answered her and Zoë's sullen expression didn't waver.

"Why isn't this wonderful?"

Again silence.

"Now I'm really confused." Dinora looked around desperately.

"It *is* good news, Dinora," said Seymour. "Aren't you happy about it, Zoë?"

"I guess," she mumbled.

"Will someone please just tell me what's going on?" Dinora pleaded.

Zoë and Seymour looked at each other. "Shall I?" Seymour asked.

Zoë glared at him. "I'll tell them," she snapped. "If you told them you would use so many adjectives it would take all morning." She turned to face the others. "My grandmother said I couldn't come this summer. She put me on the train to Kweilin and I came here instead."

The others just stared at her. Greta regretted not getting Seymour's version. A few well-placed adjectives would have helped this announcement considerably.

"Anything you want to add?" Zoë warned, looking directly at Seymour, who had started to speak.

He shut his mouth.

"Good, then let's just drop it. Tia said I could stay. End of story." Zoë turned to Daniel. "Do you have the errand list?"

"I do," said Greta, removing it from her pocket and passing it to Zoë.

"Thanks," she mumbled before storming off.

"Do you want some company?" Dinora called.

Zoë didn't bother to look back.

The rest of the morning passed uneventfully, due in most part to the fact that Zoë had yet to return. Eventually, Dinora's natural state of jubilation could no longer be suppressed and she resumed her role as ongoing commentator on any and all proceedings no matter how insignificant or mundane they might seem. These quirky and often random observations had a heartening effect on the others and by noon they were all feeling much more like themselves again.

"Shall we have lunch at the diner?" proposed Seymour. They were packing up the remaining fruits and vegetables and loading them into the back of the truck.

"Oh, that sounds lovely!" Dinora passed the last crate to Daniel.

He couldn't help but grin at his friend's exuberance. "Dinora, you're the best."

"Quite possibly," she grinned back, without missing a beat. "Although it really depends on how you look at it. Mario always says that in any evaluation," Dinora deepened her voice to imitate the authoritative and highly logical tone of her older (and infinitely more serious) brother, "you must first establish your criteria."

The others laughed as they made their way down Main Street to *Mandy's Diner*. Greta was ravenous. Now that the worrying was over and things were returning to normal, the fact that she'd eaten so little over the past 24 hours was beginning to take its toll. As they neared the restaurant however, Greta's eyes were drawn to the end of the wharf. Zoë's willowy figure sat atop one of the pilings.

"I think I'll take mine to go," Greta said, after the waitress had taken their order. They were seated in one of the booths with fire-engine red seats, which complemented the black and white checkered floor. Soon their burgers arrived and they were relieved to have beaten the lunch crowd.

Seymour nodded to Greta then surveyed the others. "Library?"

"Most definitely," Dinora affirmed, as she carefully arranged the vegetables on her cheeseburger. She topped them off with catsup poured in the perfect shape of a heart and smiled at her achievement.

Greta didn't bother to correct them. She wrapped her food in a napkin and slipped into the assembly of hungry patrons. Once outside she made her way down the wharf and found Zoë in the same spot. She lightly tapped her on the arm and then more firmly when that didn't get the girl's attention.

"Oh, hi," Zoë said dispassionately.

"Hi." Greta opened her napkin and passed Zoë half of her burger.

"Thanks."

The girls sat in silence, eating their food and watching the water. Finally, Zoë heaved an audible sigh.

"Greta, why do things have to be so complicated?"

Greta didn't answer.

Zoë continued to take deep breaths, visibly willing herself to move beyond her misery. "Well, what's done is done. Nothing I can do about it now." She turned to Greta, smiled wanly and hopped down from her perch. "Do you want to split a chocolate malt?"

The Address

When they arrived at the diner, the others were relieved to see that Zoë's mood had lightened. The two girls were greeted warmly as they slid into the booth next to Dinora. Zoë got the attention of Mandy and made the sign she and Seymour had used since they were little. The tall, grey-haired woman nodded her understanding.

"Oh, I almost forgot—sorry, Dinora," Zoë apologized for interrupting the girl who was considerately recapping the morning's events for her. She reached into her back pocket, took out a folded envelope and handed it to Daniel. "This was in the mailbox."

He accepted the envelope and unfolded it. It bore no stamp or address, only the words:

To a friend of Daniel Sutton

"That's strange," said Seymour. "And why doesn't it have a stamp?"

"It must have been hand-delivered," Dinora explained. "Remember last summer when that letter came for Tia and it had those beautiful stamps on it— were they gardenias? I think so. Now I can't remember. They were white anyway. And so I said how nice it was that they weren't ruined by the ink from the post office and Edith said that was because it was hand-delivered. It didn't have to actually go anywhere."

"Dinora, I think that has got to be the most coherent and useful thing I've ever heard you say," Zoë said and, after a reproachful look from her cousin, followed her back-handed compliment with, "And I'm sure it won't be the last."

"Certainly," Dinora agreed. "I mean, it could hardly be the last. That would be ridiculous. It's not as if I just ramble all day long with nothing important to say. Everything someone says is important in some way, even if it's just—"

"Open it," Seymour urged, avoiding Zoë's *you-do-it-too* look.

Daniel did so and took out a small scrap of paper. He placed it on the tabletop so they could all see it. There was less written on it than on the envelope itself:

43 Old Mill Road

5

☙ The House ❧

They decided to take the horses. The address
was on the other side of The Island and riding through
forests and meadows seemed the perfect medicine for
both children and animals. Dinora, as usual, rode
Diablito, a feisty stallion with only a splash of white on
one leg to mar his coal-black coat. Other than Daniel and
Edith, who took care of him, the horse refused to be
ridden by anyone except her. Some children might brag
about this or lord it over their peers. Dinora seemed
oblivious to the matter entirely, caring only for the horse
himself and how well they got along.

Daniel led the way, setting a pace difficult for Dinora
and Diablito to follow. Instead the pair developed a
pattern of surging ahead and backtracking, to Zoë's great
irritation.

"Man, Dinora," she blurted, after Diablito sidled up
next to June-Balloon, forcing Seymour to swerve away.
"Can't you control that animal?"

"Oh, I wouldn't dare. We're free spirits!" Dinora
called back as she was whisked away once more.

Zoë muttered something indistinguishable.

Greta knew that someday she would learn to ride a horse. It was definitely on her list. But she was a pragmatic girl, and patient besides. She knew better than to fill her plate with too many plans. There was plenty of time to learn to ride and since Zoë appeared content to have her, Greta was quite happy to ride along and leave the mastery of horsemanship for another summer. This allowed her to enjoy the scenery, especially today when both the sea and the skies seemed infinite. Because of this freedom to observe, she was the first to notice the dirt road in the distance.

"Look!" she cried, pointing to a hill beyond the one they were currently descending. "Could that be it?"

"It must be." Daniel reined in Sophocles and, as the spirited gelding pranced restlessly, removed the map from his satchel. "According to this, the only road around here is Old Mill Road. We should be coming up on a stream any time now."

"I wonder where the old mill is," said Seymour. "It can't be far off."

"It burned down a long time ago. That's why they built the new mill on the other side of the island."

"Isn't it funny the old mill was actually called the *Old Mill?*" said Dinora, a far off look in her eyes. "It's almost as if they knew it was destined to die."

Zoë looked at the girl, her face expressionless.

Dinora switched subjects with an impulsive challenge. "Race you!" She and Diablito charged ahead.

The others were fast behind her, eager both to find The House and to ride without restriction. Greta held on for dear life, and her desire for learning to ride (which would have placed her on her own horse at the moment) quickly gained priority.

The horses were brought up short upon entering the wood and not finding a clear trail. Again, Daniel led them, delicately maneuvering his way around trees until they reached a bridge.

"I thought you said 'stream'," said Seymour.

"That's what the map said," replied Daniel. "It must have been older than I thought."

They stared at the water before them. It was well beyond the size of a stream and while not terribly wide, maybe ten meters at most, it raged like a horizontal waterfall.

Seymour dismounted and walked to the bridge, which consisted of two birches bound together with fraying rope, and precariously straddled the gap between where they stood and a large granite boulder halfway across the water. What looked like discarded planks from the lumber mill were pieced together on the other side, zigzagging their way to the opposite shore. The last one was missing. It appeared to be a feasible jump but looks could be deceiving, especially from their vantage point.

"We'll go upstream and see if it gets any narrower," offered Zoë, helping Greta dismount. Ten minutes later they returned with bad news. "There are some parts which pool but who knows how deep they are," said Zoë. "The horses won't cross. That's for sure."

"It was the same farther along too," said Daniel. "Looks like we'll have to leave the horses here."

After watering them, the children tied the animals to an assortment of trees.

"I'll go first." Seymour eyed the makeshift bridge with suspicion. "I'm the heaviest. If it can hold me—"

"Oh, I'm heavy enough," said Dinora, barreling through and not slowing down until she had marched across the felled birches. She continued on to the planks without breaking eye contact with the others. "You know this reminds me of a time when Dulce Maria and I—"

"Dinora!" they all shouted.

"What? What's wrong? Are you okay?"

"Watch where you're going," Daniel called, already halfway across the makeshift bridge himself. The others waited their turn until, one by one, they were reunited on the other side. The horses looked at them with curiosity, not understanding why any creature would go to such lengths to be in a place which looked no better than the one before.

Daniel took out the map and, once they got their bearings, the children were off again, in search of the mysterious address. Not long afterward, the forest thinned and they found themselves on Old Mill Road.

"This doesn't make sense," said Daniel. "According to the map we should have passed it already."

"Are you sure you're reading it correctly?" Seymour asked.

Daniel passed it to his friend, who traced his finger along the faint lines. "You're right. I wonder what happened to it."

"Maybe it's not an 'it'," Zoë suggested. "Maybe it's an address for the land itself and not a house."

"I say we go back a ways. There's probably a path or something we missed." Seymour retraced their steps and the others followed, each focusing on any detail they may have overlooked.

"Do you think this might be something?" Greta called ahead. She bent down and picked up a rusted piece of metal, once painted red. "I think it's from a mailbox."

"Yes," Zoë said. "The flag you raise to show you have mail to be picked up. But how would it have gotten out here?"

"Let's spread out," Daniel instructed and within minutes they found the mailbox itself, proudly erected in the middle of the wood. The faded lettering ended in "ton".

"Maybe this wasn't always forest," Greta said slowly, still trying to formulate her thinking. "If the mailbox was here, then the driveway would start next to it. See how the trees are sparser over there." She moved to where more sunlight was getting through the forest's canopy. "There!" she cried.

They came quickly and saw that beyond the trees lay a wild meadow smothered with flowers and shrubs in haphazard arrangement.

"And look!" she cried again, pointing to a queerly-shaped conglomerate of vegetation at the far end.

At the very top, a brick chimney was barely visible, looking for all intents and purposes like the helpless hand of a drowning person.

After staring for nearly a minute, Seymour asked, "Do you think that's it?"

"We might as well get a closer look," said Daniel.

As they made their way toward it, they began to notice small details which transformed the mass of plants into something which might have been a solid structure at some point in the far distant past. *Dilapidated*. The speed with which Greta found the word confirmed her certainty. The closer they got to The House the eerier it seemed, precisely because it gradually became more distinguishable as a place where a family must have lived but in which now only nature resided.

"Should we knock?" Zoë asked dryly.

"We'd have to find the door first," said Seymour.

"Hello? Anyone home?" Dinora called, her cheery voice dissonant in the strangeness and the stillness surrounding them.

The children looked at each other, silently considering their options.

"Okay then," said Seymour. "Who else brought their Swiss Army knife?"

Four other children reached into pockets to withdraw a bright red device. They had been caught unaware before and ever since had made it as natural a companion as the sweaters they kept on hand for cold summer nights. Working together, they surveyed The House, trying to judge where the front door might be. When then found it, Daniel used his knife to cut away the vines.

He reached for the doorknob. "Locked," he announced and none of them was surprised.

"I think we're going to have to break it," said Zoë.

"Is that your solution to everything? Brute force?" Seymour chided. "Let's look for a window."

They continued to scan the building until they came upon just that.

"Hey, it's even open a little at the bottom," Dinora said, trying to raise it. "I think we'll need a board or something." She turned to Greta. "It's all about leverage."

Greta smiled at her friend and began looking for a loose board. Moments later she heard wood cracking and Zoë rounded the corner with a partial plank in hand. Seymour's expression was a cross between disbelief and disgust.

"What?" she said. "It was rotting anyway."

To Seymour's annoyance, Zoë's board fit perfectly. After jimmying it between the lower sash and the sill, they were able to raise the window enough for a very small person to squeeze through.

They all looked at Greta.

Her eyes went wide. She shook her head violently. She gulped. She took a deep breath. "Oh, drat."

"I'm happy to try, Greta, but I'm pretty sure I won't fit," offered Dinora.

"That's all right. I'll do it. Zoë, will you hoist me up?"

Zoë used her interwoven fingers as a step and in less than a minute, Greta had entered The House. She turned back to the others. "Did anyone remember—oh!"

Greta's question was answered when Zoë produced a small metal torch from her back pocket. "Always prepared," she said, passing it through.

Greta flicked on the light and gasped at what she saw.

"What? What? What is it?" Dinora's voice was the loudest but the others were just as insistent.

"I don't even know how to describe it," Greta started. "It's a . . . mess." This was easily the most useless word she could have found to describe what she saw.

Still, with so many words clamoring to be used—disheveled, damaged, deteriorated, disaster—she'd be there all afternoon trying to choose. *And those are just the "D's".* What she saw was indescribable. Quickly but carefully, she made her way through the rubble to the front door. She unlocked it and used both hands to jerk it open. With the others pushing from the opposite side, they were gradually able to make their way through.

Once inside, they all stared, dumbstruck.

It was as if someone's life had been frozen in time and then utterly destroyed. The front parlor had an armchair with an afghan quilt draped over the back. Next to it was a small table with an empty teacup, a pair of reading glasses and a folded up newspaper. Other than these, the entire room looked as if it had been hit by a cyclone. Books were strewn about, furniture tipped over, rugs hauled out of the way.

In wonder, the children moved to the next room and the next—each one mirroring the first in its chaotically-ruined state. Now that her fear had descended from terror to trepidation, Greta was noticing more than just the damage. Like the scent. The house smelled like forest—as if it had been decaying so long that nature had simply reclaimed it.

A loud crack sounded behind them and they reeled toward the noise. Daniel's foot had fallen through a rotted step as he'd tried to make his way upstairs. Greta shone the light up at him. Even with the brightness, he didn't blink.

"Danny?" Dinora asked. "Are you okay?"

He didn't respond, just stared blankly back at them.

"Daniel?" This time it was Seymour who spoke as he started up the stairs. He stopped when he realized they wouldn't hold him.

"I, I . . ." Daniel stammered. "I think I've been here before."

"When?" Zoë asked. "This place has been abandoned forever."

"I don't know. It's weird. I feel. . . . It looks vaguely familiar. I think I used to live here."

"What?" Zoë shrieked.

"Shhh!" Dinora shushed.

"Why?" she asked indignantly.

"I don't know. This place gives me the creeps. Something just doesn't feel right—like we're not supposed to be here."

"Don't be such a melvin."

But Dinora was not the only one to feel ill at ease. Even though it was sunny and warm outside, the dense foliage and overgrown shrubbery masked the sunlight and turned The House into a dark and dreary place. With no electricity, they were barely able to find their way.

Daniel wrestled his leg free and they quickly moved to the last room, probably the kitchen and hopefully, like most New England houses, it included a side entrance. They were all eager to leave.

The kitchen fit right in with the rest of The House except for more windows which let in a modicum of light.

"What in the world happened here?" Seymour murmured.

"Let's go," pleaded Dinora. "Please, let's go."

They made for the exit with Seymour in the lead. He unlocked the kitchen door and began cutting a way out.

"Wait a second," called Daniel. He was standing at the far counter. "Zoë, pass me the torch, will you?"

"What is it?" she asked, handing it to him.

"It's a package," he said in a half-whisper. "And it's addressed to me."

6

❧ The Contents ❧

By the time dinner was over, the children could barely contain their excitement.

"You kids have some place you need to be?" asked Edith dryly, after they all declined dessert, even Dinora.

"Edith, dear, don't tease them. They're excited. Darlings, you can eat dessert anytime you like. Anytime you like. You go off and do whatever it is you are so eager to do. Really, you look like a bunch of jittery jackrabbits sitting there like that."

En masse, the children rose, took their dishes and started to clean the kitchen.

"Don't mind about that," Tia called from the other room. "I'll not have you breaking my best china."

Five sets of feet sprinted up the back stairs. Once inside the boys' room, Daniel raced to the table where they'd placed the box. The others crowded around him. Seymour brought over a brighter lamp and set it on the end of the table. They could all see clearly now.

"It looks so old," said Dinora.

"I'm surprised it lasted this long," said Zoë. "You'd think in that house everything would've been ruined."

"The thing I found to be the most strange was the table in the living room," said Seymour.

"I know! The way the glasses and the teacup just sat there, like someone vanished without a trace," said Zoë.

"Abducted by aliens from a far off galaxy," Dinora mused dramatically.

"*You're* from a far off galaxy," Zoë said under her breath.

"It was definitely very . . ." Seymour began.

"Unsettling?" Greta suggested.

He nodded. "Exactly."

"Danny, how are you doing?" Dinora asked.

"Oh, I don't know." He shook his head as if to empty the thoughts clogging it. "The more I think about it, the more I realize it can't possibly be true."

"You mean about living there?"

"Yes. It doesn't make sense. I didn't even grow up near here. *The Brewster Boys Home* is 100 kilometers away, at least."

"Maybe it was from before you went there," Dinora suggested. "Before your parents passed away."

"Not likely. They were from Brewster also. There's paperwork and everything."

"Then how did you end up with Tia?" Seymour asked.

"I don't know. She just showed up one day and went into the director's office. An hour later they came and got me. Told me to pack and that I'd be spending the summer here. When September came, Tia asked me if I wanted to stay."

"You must have felt like you'd won the lottery," said Dinora. "I'd love to live here all year-round."

"To tell you the truth, I didn't feel much of anything. It took a long time to forget all the stuff that happened to me. *The Brewster Boys Home* was not an easy place to grow up. It wasn't until the next summer that I even remember laughing again."

"That was my first summer!"

Daniel blushed and Greta wondered if he shared her appreciation of Dinora's exuberant spirit and its healing powers. "Anyway, since I had never been to The Island before I was ten, I can hardly have lived there. Still. . . ."

"Let's open it! May we, Danny? Oh, do let's open it," Dinora begged excitedly.

Daniel looked up at the others and pulled open his knife. "Here's to mysteries."

The tape came off easily and soon he was folding back the flaps of a small cardboard box. They all held their breath as Daniel pushed the box closer to the light.

The very first thing he removed was a light blue baby blanket. As he took it, a silver rattle slipped out and tumbled back into the box. Daniel retrieved it and set both on the table. He reached for the remaining two items, each concealed in long white envelopes. They were bundled together with two rubber bands. Seymour took the now empty box and set it on the floor as Daniel unbound the envelopes. The first was unmarked. The second read:

Only to be opened by Daniel Sutton

"I feel like I shouldn't open it," said Daniel, softly. "This is all so strange. I keep thinking there's something I am supposed to know. But each time I try to focus on it, it's lost."

"Like when you see something in your peripheral vision but when you turn to look at it straight on, it's not there anymore?"

"Precisely, Greta."

"Do you think we shouldn't have opened the box?" Seymour asked. "It did have your name on it, after all."

Daniel was fingering the satiny edge of the baby blanket, his brow furrowed in contemplation. He set aside the envelope addressed to him specifically and reached for the blank one.

"Hey," Zoë stopped him. "I just thought of another thing that's strange." They all looked at her. "The box is addressed to Daniel but inside there's a letter which is not only addressed to him but makes a point of saying it's to be opened *only* by him."

"Almost as if the person knew it wouldn't be Daniel opening the box," Seymour finished. "Why would someone address something to a person they thought wouldn't open it. It doesn't make any sense."

"Wait," said Greta, with rare forcefulness. They froze and watched as she internally grappled with something. "There's another thing."

They waited.

"The newspaper," she said, her tense expression replaced with a triumphant grin.

"Of course!" Seymour cried and the others shushed him, not knowing why but somehow inherently sensing this was a puzzle which required not only focus but quiet.

"The newspaper can tell us how long the box has been there," explained Greta.

"But we didn't look for the date," Zoë said.

"No." Greta was still smiling. "But I did see part of the headline."

"What was it?" Daniel asked.

"It was about Eisenhower."

"The president?" asked Dinora.

"Obviously," said Zoë. "Daniel, if he was president when the box was put there, then you would have been—"

"Just a baby, or maybe not even born," figured Seymour.

"Now I'm no expert but I'm pretty sure you can't send something to someone who hasn't been born yet," proclaimed Dinora confidently. "I think it's illegal."

"Oh, good grief." Zoë rolled her eyes.

"Do you think they were *sending* it or that it was sent *there*?" asked Seymour.

The Contents

Daniel picked up the box and put it back on the table, folding the flaps to see the cover. "Just the name," he confirmed. "It could have been either."

"I wonder why it got left in the kitchen," said Greta.

"There's something weird about that too." Daniel looked up from the baby blanket he was unconsciously gripping in his left hand. "The whole house was a mess but the box was placed neatly, almost precisely, on the counter. It even looked like someone had cleared off the counter in order to place the box there." He paused. "If you were that messy, why would you even care?"

"I think the person who lived there wasn't messy," said Greta. "The table next to the armchair. It was so . . . orderly."

"Dishes!" Dinora exclaimed, earning another round of shushing. "Dishes," she repeated in a whisper.

"What about them?" Zoë grumbled.

"There weren't any dishes in the sink. There were dishes in the drying rack though. If I were a messy person—" She turned to Greta. "Which I'm not, thank you very much. But if I were, then I'd never wash my dishes. I'd just let them pile up and get dirtier and dirtier."

"She makes a valid point," said Zoë.

The glow of pride on Dinora's face could have lit the room.

"What about this," Seymour started. "The person who lives there—albeit there could be more than one—is neat. Then someone comes along and messes up the place. After that someone else comes and leaves the box."

"Delivers the box," Zoë corrected.

"Huh?"

"Delivers. You don't just *leave* a box. If the box was brought *to* The House then it would have been brought there for a reason. I think Daniel did live there and that's *why* the box was delivered there."

"Wouldn't it be fascinating if the person who messed up The House was messing it up because they were looking *for* the box," Dinora said conspiratorially. "But the other person knew they were going to do that and so waited until the first chap left before bringing it. That's what happened on an episode of *Mis Secretos*," Dinora sat back smugly, clearly proud of her theory.

"Dinora, this is not one of your stupid *novellas*," Zoë chided.

"It is possible though," Seymour said.

"Hmph," grunted Zoë.

"Okay," Daniel said resolutely. "I'm going to do it." Not giving himself time to change his mind, he quickly ripped open the first envelope and reached inside. It was a ferry schedule. Taped to the front was a ticket stub.

"Why would someone want to send Danny that?" Dinora looked confused. "He can't even use the ticket now."

Daniel hesitated briefly before opening the second envelope—the one intended solely for him. A key tumbled out.

Seymour picked it up and held it under the light. "It's a bank key," Seymour said, squinting to read some writing. "For *Belfast Savings & Loan*." He handed the key to Daniel. "It must be for a safety deposit box."

7

❧ The Owner ❧

Although the children stayed up well into the night, none of them had any trouble waking the next morning. Energized by their plans, they bounded downstairs to find that Tia had once again laid out a delectable breakfast. This clear indicator that all had returned to normal was heartily welcomed and provided an unneeded, but certainly appreciated, boost.

It was such a beautiful day they decided to pack a picnic lunch and hike into town. They didn't know how long their investigations might take but Dinora easily convinced them an *al fresco* lunch would be just the thing.

The children distributed the supplies into backpacks but decided to leave the contents of the mysterious box at Tia's. Except for the key, nothing was of value. Who would care about a few scraps of paper and some old baby stuff? But just in case they were important, Daniel hid the box on the highest closet shelf so Tia wouldn't accidentally throw it away.

An hour later they neared the outskirts of the village. They could see the town green in the center, bordered by various buildings on all sides. The First Congregational

Church secured one end and was mirrored on the other by the town hall. Both two-story white buildings served as bookends for the village and looked to Greta much like two lighthouses amid a sea of shops. Beyond all of this was the Penobscot Bay, which didn't have enough energy to do more than glisten under the morning sun.

"Good thing it's Friday," said Daniel. "Everything should be open."

They chose to split up, figuring it might take awhile to find what they needed. Upon reaching Main Street, Seymour and Greta headed off to the library with the assurance that they'd meet up with the others by the gazebo at noon.

Dinora was in charge of the *Island Ad-Vantages*, the town's newspaper. She was unanimously elected for this portion of the plan since it required a ditzy charm no one else could have delivered nearly as well. Dinora wasn't insulted in the least by this, happy to help in any way she could. Further, she liked the idea of sitting in the corner of an air-conditioned office, scrolling through four years of microfiche. And in little more than twenty minutes, she had gracefully fibbed her way into doing just that.

Although it definitely wouldn't have been her first choice of how to spend a summer morning, she was committed to their cause of solving the mystery. *Dinora Enriquez and the Case of the Weird Box*, she considered as she opened the first container in the stack. *No,* she thought, *Detective Dinora and the Mysterious Stuff inside the Really Weird Box.* She liked that one much better.

There was another reason she was glad to take on this task. Dinora was absolutely certain that if her brother were here, this would be the first assignment he'd want for himself and the *last* one he'd want for her. Mario was a reasonable person who valued sound logic. According to their father, Dinora was much more "instinctual" and whenever he said so, Dinora noticed there was always a slight pause before the word. Apparently, this was some hidden joke between the two of them but Dinora didn't get what was so funny. Mario was also incredibly patient. For a chemist, this was crucial. And as in practically every other respect, Dinora was the complete opposite. Not only did she not see anything particularly useful in patience, her lack of attention to detail and tendency to daydream would have made Mario cringe at the thought of her on this assignment.

I'll show him, she thought. *I'll be the epitome of patience and attention. I'll be the perfect scientist. I'll notice every detail. I'll find . . .* "Uh, oh," she finished aloud.

"Everything all right over there, dear?" the secretary asked.

"Yes," Dinora answered dejectedly. "I just got distracted for a moment." She sighed heavily and took the twenty or so plastic strips she'd already "checked" and returned them to her "to be checked" pile. She rubbed her eyes and started again, her determination renewed. *I'll find something useful and when the others tell Mario, he'll say, "Dinora—"*

She stopped mid-thought. "Oh, dear. I've done it again."

Greta and Seymour weren't having much more luck in the library. Looking through census records, family trees and the minutes taken in town hall meetings was boring, even to Greta.

"I hope Dinora, Daniel and Zoë are having more luck than we are," Seymour said, reaching for another volume.

And in truth, Daniel and Zoë were about to have quite a bit of luck.

"I'd like to see the property records for a house on Old Mill Road," Daniel said to the elderly man behind the counter. They'd been sent here from the office down the hall which they'd visited upon the instructions of the Town Clerk on the floor below.

"Terribly sorry, young man but all these files are confidential."

"Then why is it called the 'Office of Public Records'?" Zoë demanded insolently. She had not taken kindly to the constant redirection and red tape which had filled up most of their morning.

"That is not a very ladylike tone, missy," the man retorted, mustache twitching.

"Neither is yours," Zoë snapped back.

"Sir," Daniel pleaded. "*Is* this the Office of Public Records?"

"I suppose."

"Hmph," Zoë snorted.

"So then these records are, in fact, public."

"I suppose."

"And do you keep property records here?"

"I suppose."

"And may I please see the property records for 43 Old Mill Road?"

"Why?"

"Oh, you are a real piece of work," Zoë accused.

"Excuse me?" asked Daniel.

"Why do you want to see them?" the man asked indignantly.

"Is he required by law to tell you?"

"I suppose not."

Zoë gripped the edge of the counter and leaned forward, menacingly. "Then why don't you just go get the file before I climb over this counter and show you just how—"

"All right, all right," said the man, scampering away.

"Wow." Daniel stared at her. "I can't believe that worked."

Zoë stepped back from the counter and shook her head. "Neither can I."

The two stood in their bemused state until the man returned, a few minutes later, with a manila file in his hand.

"You have to look at it where I can see you," he glared at Zoë. "And that's the law!"

"Fine, fine," she responded. "No need to get snippy."

The man grumbled intelligibly as he passed the file to the children and motioned to a bench where they could peruse the contents and still be within eyesight.

They sat and opened the file gingerly. The first piece of paper unfolded into a large map delineating property lines. The second, equally large, was a faded cobalt blue with white lines going every which way.

"Will you look at that," Zoë said. "Blueprints are actually 'blue prints'." She paused before asking, "Did I just sound like Dinora?"

"A little," laughed Daniel.

The last piece of paper was titled *Proprietor History*. Zoë traced her finger down the column.

"So who owns it?" Daniel asked impatiently.

"Well, Daniel my boy," Zoë smiled. "According to this . . . you do."

"What?"

"Look, here you are, right at the bottom. Current owner: Daniel R. Sutton."

Daniel stared at the paper.

"Congratulations, Daniel," Zoë said wryly. "That's almost as good as inheriting a hernia."

Daniel sat speechless but there was clearly plenty going on in his head.

"So what's the 'R' stand for? You can tell me," Zoë teased. "Is it 'Rupert'?"

"Huh? Oh. I don't know," he stammered.

"How can you not know your own name?"

He turned to her. "Zoë, it's not my name. My middle name is Lewis. This isn't me. I think the box wasn't meant for me either. What in the world is going on?"

It was half past noon when Zoë and Daniel joined the others. Everyone except a dazed Daniel was eager to report first. At the same time they were dying to know what the others had discovered. In the mêlée that followed, it became clear that each group had at least found something, and all were satisfied the day's adventure had been a fruitful one. Knowing they'd eventually get their turn to share not only what they'd learned but the equally interesting story of *how* they'd learned it, put them more at ease.

At an empty picnic table by the wharf, they laid out their lunch. It was a marvelous feast but no match for the hungry children. They unpacked fresh bread, salami, cherry tomatoes, cucumbers and Cavendish strawberries from the garden. To top it all off, they each had a ginger beer kept cold through Daniel's clever packing strategies. Now that they were eating, no one seemed quite so interested in going first, as their attention had shifted to their simple but scrumptious meal.

"Well, I guess I'll get mine over with." Daniel stood as if he were about to address the shareholders at an important board meeting. "My friends, we discovered, through hours upon hours of bureaucracy, that The House belongs to one Daniel R. Sutton but—"

"Oh, Danny, that's wonderful!" Dinora interrupted.

"How?" Zoë scoffed. "It's a dump."

"Unfortunately, or perhaps fortunately, I am not Daniel R. Sutton. Ladies and gentleman, I am Daniel L. Sutton," he said with a flourish. His bravado quickly faded. "The box isn't mine either. It was wrong of me to open it."

"But you remembered The House," insisted Dinora.

"Who knows why? Probably I imagined it."

"Not necessarily," Seymour said, taking the stage as Daniel returned to the table. "Greta, tell him what you found?"

"You can do it," Greta said humbly.

"Very well then. Daniel, will you please confirm that your mother's name was Felicia Sutton?"

"How did you know?"

"Then it's true?" Greta asked, tears beginning to well up in her eyes.

"Yes, why? What's going on?"

Greta took his hand, "Daniel, Felicia's father was Daniel Rutherford Sutton. He was your grandfather."

It took a minute for this to sink in. "But I was told there was no one. They told me that. At the home, they said that. Even on my records, it says, 'no living relatives'."

"It could have been that he had already died," said Seymour.

"I always thought I had no family," Daniel said. "After the car crash—"

"What car crash?" Dinora asked.

"The one that killed my parents when I was four. That's when I went to *The Brewster Boys Home*."

"Daniel, do you remember any of it?" asked Greta. "Anything before you went there?"

"Not really. I have a few vague pictures in my head but most of what I know is from my record, or what the staff told me."

"Danny, I think they lied to you. Or maybe someone lied to them," Dinora said.

"What makes you say that?"

"I found something in an old newspaper," she paused. "Danny, it was an obituary."

"For my grandfather?"

"No, your mother."

"And it didn't mention the car crash?"

"I think there wasn't any crash. The obituary said she died from the influenza."

"What?"

"There was something else," Dinora continued. "It said that she was survived by only two family members: her father and her infant son. Danny, you were only three at the time."

That afternoon and the entire next day the children scoured the town for information. Little more was to be found however, and in the end, it was clear they'd have to expand their search.

"We need a bigger library," Greta voiced what they all knew to be true. "Any suggestions?"

"There's a library in Belfast," Zoë said. "I think it's near the *Belfast Savings & Loan.*"

The others considered the opportunities of such a trip.

"I don't know," Daniel said hesitantly.

"You're not simply dying to find out what's in the safety deposit box, Danny? If I were you, I'd be exploding by now. You're not even a little curious? Even a little?" Dinora punctuated this last question with fingers a centimeter apart and he smiled.

"Of course I'm curious. But it doesn't feel honest. It doesn't belong to me."

"Legally it does," Seymour said. "Or at least one could make that case. You don't know where your grandfather is but presumably he's no longer alive, in which case, you are the only living relative. You get everything."

"Hooray!" Zoë said sarcastically. "You've won a creepy run-down cottage and—wait for it—a key."

"Okay," he said. "I get it. I know you're right. There's still something that doesn't fit though. I keep wondering where I might have been the year before I went to the home."

"Well, if your grandfather was alive at the time, you probably went with him," said Seymour.

"And that's why you remembered The House. You must have lived there with him," Dinora said.

"But then what happened?"

They were all silent, each thinking of the only thing that could have happened.

"I don't even remember him," whispered Daniel, using his hands to wipe tears away. "I always held out hope, you know? I thought maybe I'd find some relative, somewhere. And now even that's gone. There's no doubt. I have no one."

"You have us, Danny." But even Dinora knew this was not the same.

8

✥ The Church ✥

The next morning bloomed brightly.

"When I was younger," Dinora told the others at breakfast, "I used to think Sunday was called 'sun-day' because it was always sunny." She laughed nervously before turning to Greta and whispering, "It's not."

"Come, children, come. No rest for the wicked. No rest indeed," Tia tittered as she raced through the dining room and into the kitchen. She must have been dressed to the nines but all Greta saw was a bright fuchsia blur and what looked to be a peacock feather.

"Did you get a look at that hat?" Zoë asked. She herself was dressed for church in navy blue slacks (the closest thing to jeans Tia would allow) and a white blouse.

"I know!" Dinora agreed wholeheartedly. "It was magnificent! I wonder if she has another. Tia?" Dinora raced after her.

Once it was established that the over-the-top chapeau was a one-of-a-kind, they all piled into Tia's Sunday car—an aquamarine *Ford Fairlane*. With Greta and Zoë sharing a seatbelt there was enough room for the five children and Tia. Edith never went to church.

Once arrived, the children were greeted like royalty. A congregation, with an average age of seventy, was always delighted to see young people, especially the first Sunday of summer.

"Oh, Miss Witherspoon, good morning," called Emily Eaton, the minister's extroverted wife. "Your hat is simply divine." Her initial salutation and compliment given, Mrs. Eaton got right down to business. "Now, before I forget—"

"Not very likely," Zoë said into her sleeve.

"—the Ladies Aid Society is hosting a Monte Carlo Night. Isn't that perfectly scandalous? Well, of course, all the proceeds will go to the Steeple Fund. And we were just discussing who would be the best person to—"

"Excuse me," Zoë slipped past the two women and the others followed.

They greeted their way through to Tia's pew, halfway down on the right. Tia always said, "The back row is for busybodies and the only reason to sit in the front is to make everyone notice your new hat. Whether it's nosiness or vanity, it has no place in the Lord's house. No place 't all."

As Reverend Eaton began the invocation, Dinora leaned over Greta to poke Zoë. "Psst."

Zoë ignored her.

"Psst," she repeated.

"What is it?" Zoë mouthed.

"Someone's looking at you," she smiled and batted her eyelashes.

"What are you talking about?"

"Look," Dinora nodded her head to the other side of the aisle and back a row. Greta and Zoë turned and just as they did, a boy with tousled dirty-blonde hair re-routed his attention to the preacher.

"Dinora, you are such a girl," Zoë admonished.

"He sure is pretty," Dinora said.

"I didn't notice."

"Well he noticed you. He hasn't taken his eyes off you since we arrived."

"Which would mean *you* haven't taken your eyes off *him* since we arrived."

"Amen!" Tia's words said one thing but her tone was entirely different. The subject of the boy was dropped and the girls behaved themselves for the rest of the service.

Afterward, as they lined up to greet the pastor, Dinora resumed her investigation.

"I wonder who he is. My, he's certainly dreamy. Look there, Zoë. He has all those girls doting on him and he only has eyes for you. Oh, it's so exciting. Just like in that episode of *Mis Secretos* when Don Pablo first notices Alicia and—"

"Oh, for Pete's sake, Dinora. Will you just let it—"

"Hi." It was the boy.

Zoë stopped mid-sentence. "Uh . . . hi."

"How do you do?" Dinora boomed, reaching for his hand and pumping it vigorously. "I'm Dinora. This is Greta and *this* is Zoë. Ouch!" Dinora rubbed her foot.

"Nice to meet you," he said, shaking each girl's hand in turn. "I'm Eli. You're staying with Miss Witherspoon for the summer, right?"

"Yes we are!" Dinora's enthusiasm had returned in full force. "Seymour too. He's the big one over there talking with Mrs. Damon. He's quite musical. And Danny's around here somewhere but you probably already know him. He'll be a freshman in the fall. What year are you?"

The boy started laughing. "Um, I'll be a junior and yes, I know Daniel and I'm glad Seymour's musical."

"Hah!" This last part got a laugh out of Zoë.

"Oh, so she does speak." Eli turned his gaze to her and smiled easily. Greta had to admit that Dinora was right. The boy was indeed . . . *comely*. "For a second there

I thought Dinora might be the official mouthpiece for the group."

"Oh, she's a mouthpiece all right," said Zoë.

"It's true. Sometimes I get going and I just can't seem to stop. For example, one time I was with Dulce Maria—she's my best friend during the school year—and I started explaining—"

"Oh, Eli, there you are!" A gaggle of girls descended upon them, led by a perfectly quaffed brunette wearing too much makeup. "I've been looking for you everywhere."

"And now you've found me. Ivy, I'd like you to meet Dinora, Zoë and Greta."

"Yes," she condescended. "Happy to make your acquaintance. Now Eli, we were just talking with your mother about the church picnic and how it would be simply lovely if the boys—"

"Yeah, well. We have to go," Zoë interrupted, linking her arms with the other two and closing the considerable gap in the receiving line. In fact, Tia was already there, visiting with Reverend and Mrs. Eaton about the service and the weather and all things ecclesiastical.

"Wait, I wanted—" Eli called after them, much to the annoyance of Ivy and her chorus.

"Eli, don't be so rude. I was in the middle of telling you how—"

"Sorry, Ivy. I'll be right back." He started walking away from her. "But hold that thought. It sounds fascinating."

Ivy stood there, mouth agape until one of her friends closed it for her.

Mrs. Eaton was about to finish enlisting Tia when Eli joined them. "And here's my Eli. Dear, you remember Miss Witherspoon."

"Of course, Mother," he nodded to Tia. "It's nice to see you, Miss Witherspoon."

"And these lovely girls are Zoë, Dinora and—oh my, I can never remember the little one."

"Greta," Zoë said, not trying in the least to hide her disapproval.

"Oh yes, of course and little Greta."

"Yes, Mother. We've met. In fact, I was just about to invite them to the dance on Saturday."

"Oh yes, you simply must come. It's a whale of a good time."

"We're busy," said Zoë definitively.

"But there's always time for dancing!" Dinora beamed conspiratorially at Eli. "We'd love to come!"

"Let's be clear about this," Zoë said exceedingly slowly. She was centimeters away from Dinora's wide-eyed face. It was Sunday evening and they were back in Tia's grand library. Seymour and Daniel had gathered what little information the children had been able to find and were reviewing these clues on the large mahogany table. Greta was sifting through Tia's books, shelf by shelf, in search of anything which might be useful. Zoë was sulking and Dinora hadn't stopped rambling about a variety of romantic scenarios since that morning.

After hours of silence, Zoë's words—as hushed as they were—got everyone's attention. "I am going to say this once, Dinora, and *only* once. There is no way I am going to set foot in that crummy hall this Saturday, no way I am going to dress up like some tart and there's no way I am going to dance with that boy, no matter how 'dreamy' he is. And if you don't stop talking about it this instant I am going to spend the rest of my life in search of something that annoys you almost as much as you annoy me and once I find it I won't stop doing it . . ." She paused and Greta thought it wasn't so much for effect as in effort not to lose control of her temper entirely. Her last word was barely audible. ". . . *ever.*"

The Church

There were many things Greta loved about Dinora. Above all of them was her resilient spirit. Zoë's threat, issued in all seriousness, would have intimidated anyone. Even Greta shuddered a little at the intensity. Not Dinora. She simply smiled complacently as she mimed the zipping of her lips and throwing away the key, all with a knowing twinkle in her eye.

"There's a dance?" Seymour asked Daniel.

"I'll tell you about it later. In the meantime I think we should go to Belfast tomorrow. We can visit the library, check out any other records at the courthouse and . . ." He took a moment to make sure it was what he wanted. ". . . and I can go see what that safety deposit box holds for me."

"How will we get there," Greta asked, "if you can't drive the truck off The Island? Will we ask Tia, or Edith?"

"Daniel leaned back in his chair and put his feet up on the table. "I thought we'd sail."

This got Zoë's immediate attention. "Now *that*," she said, casting a disparaging look at Dinora, "is what I call a *good* idea."

9

∂ The Bank ∂

After checking and rechecking everything, Daniel pronounced *The Prudence* sea-ready. This time boarding went more easily for Greta, and even though she was a little queasy, she took great pride in the fact that she didn't pass out. Zoë was at the helm with Daniel at the pulpit keeping an eye out for rocks. Especially in the early morning fog which blanketed them, these could be difficult to see and hazardous to hit. When they were at a safe enough distance, Zoë cut the engine and Seymour helped her with the heavy mainsail. Once raised, it had an immediate and therapeutic effect on the girl.

Seymour held the map but it wasn't the same as navigating on dry land. Zoë took a try but eventually it was Daniel, who found their destination. Zigzagging against a strong headwind, the trip took them close to three hours.

"It'll be much quicker on the way back, sailing downwind," said Daniel. "But we should still plan to leave no later than three o'clock, which gives us about four hours."

The Bank

They had dropped their anchor off shore and were using the rubber dinghy to finish the trip. After landing and securing the boat, they made their way into the center of town and decided to divide into two groups. Daniel and Seymour would visit *Belfast Savings & Loan* while the girls researched at the public library.

"Good luck, Danny," Dinora hugged him impulsively.

"Thanks, Dinora." His anxiety was palpable.

Greta thought he looked like he was, at best, having second thoughts and, at worst, ready to vomit. "It'll be okay," she offered pathetically. "You've every right to open it."

"Yeah, I guess. C'mon, Seymour." The two left the girls and made their way to the bank.

"I have a proposal," Greta spoke with more authority than she felt. The truth was, she wasn't exactly thrilled to be stuck with the "dueling duo", as she'd nicknamed them in her head. She knew if she didn't take charge, then the time would pass without them accomplishing anything, other than further frustrating Zoë. "We're looking for information on The House and on Daniel's grandfather. We should start with old newspapers." Greta walked purposefully as she talked, thankful the other two were following so compliantly. She quickened her pace, fearful of losing momentum. "We don't have much time. We need to find any noteworthy events that might have taken place between the date Daniel's mother died and the date he went to *The Brewster Boys Home*."

By the time she finished her instructions, they had arrived at the library, which felt like home turf, even if Greta had never visited this particular one before. She went straight to the research department. In less than ten minutes, the three girls were lined up in a row, looking into microfiche machines at a year's worth of headlines from the *Bangor Daily News*.

"I'm seeing a lot of stuff on the influenza," Dinora said.

"So am I," echoed Greta. "This article says more than 36,000 people died that year."

"And we still don't have a cure," Zoë added cynically. "Probably twice that many are dying now."

"And it's not just old people or people who are already sick. It's young people too, like Danny's mother. And babies."

"Here's something," Greta said. "Oh, dear."

"What?" The other girls abandoned their stations to join her.

"It's a story about a Sutton family." Greta's eyes still focused on the machine. "There's a picture of a Daniel Sutton but he's old."

"Then it must be his grandfather," said Dinora. "Does he look like Danny?"

"I don't know. He might. The picture's awfully grainy."

"What's the article about?" Zoë insisted.

Greta slowly stood. "See for yourself."

Zoë sat down on the vacated seat and peered through the eyeholes. "Oh, hector!"

"What?" demanded Dinora.

Zoë didn't respond, just kept reading. Finally, she looked up. "You two stay here and wait for the boys. I need to go check something out. If they get back before I do, I'll meet you at the dinghy as soon as I'm done." She ran past a scolding librarian and plowed through the heavy wooden doors.

"I wonder what that was all about," said Greta.

But the other girl wasn't listening. She was immersed in the article, tears streaming down her face.

Less than an hour later Zoë and the boys arrived, each one with a look of fear or worry upon their face. The fact that they were coming from different places was even more troubling to Greta, as it invariably meant bad news doubled. Daniel, in particular, looked as if he were about to either cry or scream uncontrollably at any minute.

"We need to leave," Seymour said, turning around and guiding Daniel, who clearly could have been led anyplace and not been aware of it. The girls were right behind them. No one spoke as they walked toward the shore. Greta noticed that, despite the sense of urgency, they were walking and not running. Seymour was in the lead and set a deliberately casual pace. *He doesn't want us to be noticed*, she thought. Then she remembered where the boys had just been and saw the black briefcase Seymour was carrying. This struck her as peculiar. *Why does he have it, and not Daniel?*

Once on the outskirts of town, Daniel himself took a considerable lead. The others could barely keep up and when they arrived at the dinghy, he'd already untied it. They scrambled into the little craft, rocking it precariously in the process. Seymour used an oar to shove off, before replacing it in the oarlock and focusing all of his strength on rowing. It wasn't until they had raised the anchor and the mainsail that Daniel spoke. There was a look of panic in his eyes and tenseness in his shoulders that hadn't been there before his visit to *Belfast Savings & Loan*.

"We went to the bank," he started. "It was so easy. I just showed them my driver's permit. They let us into the room, took out the box and left. All I had to do was unlock it."

"What was in it?" Dinora asked.

"Show them," Daniel told Seymour, turning away in disgust.

Seymour reached into the pocket of his jacket and pulled out a small piece of paper. The wind wrestled with it as he passed it to the girls. Together they gripped it so it wouldn't fly away.

I know you don't want this and you despise me for what I did to get it, but here's your half.
P.

"Danny, what does that mean? Despised for doing what? Why would—"

"Whatever it was, it was something bad." He shifted the sail and the sloop picked up speed. Daniel glanced back at Seymour. "Show them what's in the briefcase." There was an edge in his voice Greta had never heard before. "Take it down below. I've got the helm. I don't want to see it again anyway."

They crowded into the cabin and Seymour set the black briefcase on the small kitchen countertop. "This was all," he said softly, pausing to unlock the silver latches. The top popped open. "The note, and this." He pulled it back so the others could see clearly. It was money. A lot of it.

"How much?" Zoë asked flatly.

"I didn't have time to count it all. Daniel was getting pretty worked up and it was all I could do to get him out of there before he completely fell apart. He didn't even want to take the money." Seymour ran his hand through his curly blonde hair, wilder now from the wind. "It's a lot though—well over a hundred thousand."

They gasped.

"We need to tell Daniel something," Zoë blurted.

"Zo, wait. He's had enough for one day. This really upset him. Wait until he calms down. It's better that way."

"No," Greta said. "She's right. He should know this. It might make sense of the money and it won't be any easier to hear later."

"Is it bad?" Seymour knew the answer but was still holding out hope.

The girls nodded in unison.

"Very," said Zoë.

They emerged from the cabin.

The Bank

One look at their somber expressions and Daniel said, "Tell me." He sounded like he thought things couldn't get any worse, but were about to anyway.

"We found an article, Daniel," Greta started. "About your grandfather."

"Did it say how he died?" Daniel's voice was cold and brittle.

"He's not dead, Daniel," Zoë said calmly. The other girls looked at her in surprise. "I went to the courthouse to make sure," she explained.

"Then where is he? Why did he leave me?"

Dinora started to cry. "I'm sorry, Danny."

"What? What is it?"

"Daniel, he's alive . . . but he's in jail," Zoë said with sympathetic evenness.

"In jail?" he asked incredulously. "In jail? For what? Dinora, *for what?*"

Dinora gulped before whispering, "Murder."

The man picked up the phone. "Yes?"

"Sir, this is Alfred Noonan, from *Belfast Savings & Loan.*"

"Yes?"

"Sir, box 1461 has been opened."

A pause before, "Thank you, Alfred."

"Is there anything else you'll be needing, sir?"

"No, Alfred, that will be—actually, Alfred, could you describe the man to me?"

"It was a boy, sir, maybe fourteen or fifteen."

"A boy?"

"Yes, sir"

"A boy? And did he give his name?"

"Of course. It was Daniel Sutton."

"Daniel Sutton? That's not possible."

"I'm quite certain, sir."

10

❧ The Suitor ❧

When they arrived home Daniel went immediately to his room. He didn't come out for the rest of the evening and since he had made the others promise not to tell what had happened, they tried their best to avoid the topic altogether.

"I see," said Edith, in a way that made the children feel like she really did see and that was the problem. Still, both Tia and Edith let the subject rest. They were neither of them ones to intrude on others' business, especially when it was clear the children were safe and sound.

The four remaining children were unusually quiet as they cleaned up after dinner. Of course each of them was dying to talk but knew that whatever was said would need to be said in assured privacy. When at last they had the opportunity to return to the boys' room, where they had hidden the money, they began.

But Greta cut them off. "It's not right," she said solemnly. "We need to wait for Daniel and he's not ready yet." She motioned to the money, the note and the retrieved box of clues. "All of this can wait until the morning. So should we."

The Suitor

Since discussion was not an option, the children made their way to the music room, one of their favorite distractions. Before they knew it, the evening had passed pleasantly and they were off to bed.

In the morning, Daniel was gone.

The House seemed different this time. In the early haze of morning, just past dawn, it was ethereal and otherworldly. Daniel approached the front door and tried to imagine how it would appear if he were a meter shorter. He scanned the garden but even his best imagination couldn't picture what it must have been like when taken care of by loving hands. He paused by each of the bizarrely-planted flower beds, strewn across the large lawn. They looked comical and didn't fit with the rest of the garden.

Once in The House, it was an entirely different experience. He moved patiently, systematically through each room, trying to find something that would trigger a memory. But nothing caused more than a vague sense of familiarity and even if he did remember something, there would have been little room for it in his mind. *My grandfather. My only family. A murderer.* It sickened him to think of it and he tried not to dwell on the idea. It was a futile effort.

He couldn't remember him. *Pictures*, he thought. *There must be pictures somewhere.* The damage was worst in the small parlor where the books were kept. It definitely seemed haphazard enough to support Dinora's theory that his grandfather was not a slob but that someone was looking for something. *Evidence?* he wondered. Perhaps it *was* the box. He made his way to the books but the water had ruined all of them. Even so, he didn't find anything that resembled photographs.

Finally, he faced the real challenge—the thing he'd wanted to see most and yet dreaded seeing at the same time. As he ascended the stairs, he was careful to stay close to the wall, hoping for added support. The last thing he needed was to break his leg and, like the box, be forgotten here.

When he got to the landing, he knew which way to turn. His instincts, or more likely his memory, steered him to the left. At the end of the short hall, a door stood ajar. He opened it and the past came flooding back. The room had been destroyed but the key pieces were here. The wallpaper. He remembered someone putting it up and how happy it had made his mother. Was it his grandfather? She'd been sitting up in bed but it was afternoon. She had been sick. He remembered that, remembered someone sitting next to her, tending to her. A man. Would a murderer do these things? He made his way to the bureau and opened the top drawer.

A blaze of brown fur jumped out at him.

"Aah!" he screamed, frightened by the animal and scared again by how ghostly his own voice sounded in this room—this room of sick mothers and the murderers who cared for them.

The creature chirruped and Daniel saw it was a squirrel. He used more caution to open the other drawers. Most had clothing or bedding but the top right one contained just what he had hoped to find. *Jackpot.* It was a picture of a young woman on a swing, holding the rope with one hand and her toddler son with the other. It was the first picture of his mother he'd ever seen. He looked for another and found a framed one. It was of a man, older but somehow not old. He was wearing thick glasses and sitting in an armchair with an afghan hanging over the back. He had the same child on his lap and he held a book. The boy was excitedly pointing to one of the pages and the man was laughing. *The murderer was laughing and I was sitting in his lap.* Daniel felt bile rising in his throat. He rushed down the stairs and out the front door just in time to vomit on the overgrown wisteria. He wiped his mouth with his shirt, sickened by the metallic taste and the memories.

He ran back to the stream and washed up for nearly twenty minutes. The cold water felt wonderful as he drank, washed his shirt and dunked his head. He wanted to just dive right in. He imagined being a fish and just swimming away without a care in the world. He imagined being a boy—an orphan—cascading down a raging and rock-strewn river. If his head hit on a big enough rock, he'd be as carefree as that fish.

"You must be clean by now, Danny," Dinora called from the middle of the stream. She stood majestically on the large granite rock looking like an Aztec princess without a fear in the world. Diablito pranced on the far shore, anxious to be moving again.

"I went to The House," he said.

"That's kind of what I figured."

"It was . . ." He couldn't think of how to finish the sentence.

"That's okay," she smiled broadly. "You can tell me later. Do you feel like breakfast? Tia made scones."

Daniel stood and shook out some water from his hair. He bounded toward Dinora in long, confident strides. "I think I'll pass on breakfast," he said. "But I sure could use some company."

"Oh, we've got plenty of that. In fact, we've had quite a morning already. Don't worry, nothing about you. We all knew you'd be fine. I especially knew it." Her eyes twinkled mischievously. "These were events of a *romantic* nature."

"Eli?" Daniel asked, grateful to be talking about something other than his problems and even more grateful to be talking with Dinora.

"That's what I thought, but no. Just wait until you hear this. It's positively amazing."

As they cantered over the hills, Dinora wasn't able to go into quite as much detail as she would have liked. She had to sacrifice her own opinions in the mad desire to catch Daniel up on the latest news.

It seemed some flowers had arrived that morning.

"Heavens," Tia exclaimed. "Look at these. My, aren't they splendid? Simply splendid."

"I think I know who sent them," Dinora sang.

"Give it a rest, Dinora," growled Zoë. "Eat a cookie."

"Tia, there's a card. Oh! Well Zoë, it looks like you're off the hook," said Dinora. "They're for you, Tia."

"For me? Oh my."

"May I read the card?" Dinora asked after she'd already broken the envelope's seal. "Oh Tia, listen to this. 'Beautiful flowers for a beautiful lady'," Dinora drawled. "They're from Mr. Roy Billings."

"Billings? Edith, darling. Do I know a Billings?"

"Think 'oil', Dot," Edith said, not looking up from the morning paper.

"Oil? Oil. Oil! Yes, well, isn't that strange?" she murmured to herself.

"Tia! Who is it? You have to tell us or we'll just fall to bits," Dinora squealed with rabid fascination, although she was clearly the only one interested.

"It's Roy Billings, the Texas oil tycoon. He has a summer place on The Island. I think he may have brought me some punch at church," she paused to recollect. "Or maybe not. I don't remember. Anyway, what a sweet man to send over such lovely flowers. I mustn't forget to send a little card."

Daniel and Dinora arrived as the others were starting to work in the garden. After the events of the past few days it was precisely what Daniel needed. Working with his hands, an honest day's labor, had a cathartic effect on him. By lunchtime the children had weeded enough to last another week and harvested enough to sell the following day at the farmers market.

After lunch they raced to the Lily Pond, where they played and swam the rest of the afternoon. The evening was filled with mindless board games, music and the company of good friends who seemed to know just what Daniel needed. The day could not have been more pure and uncomplicated. It was the perfect medicine. As they readied for bed Daniel asked Seymour if he would mind some company.

"Glad to have it. It feels weird being the only boy in the *boys'* room."

"Thanks," said Daniel, and they all knew what he meant.

The market proved to be right up Dinora's alley, as both of her romantic sagas were furthered with the visit to their stall of not just one but two suitors of Witherspoon women.

Mr. Roy Billings, millionaire and bigwig, was the first to call on their modest country vegetable stand.

"And Miss Witherspoon? Is she not here with y'all today?"

"Unfortunately no, and you are?" Dinora queried innocently. Greta had no difficulty picturing the girl's future as a yenta.

"Billings is the name, little lady. Mr. Roy Billings. I have a summer place over in Sunset."

"Billings?" Dinora feigned ignorance. "Oh, why of course. You are the one who sent those lovely flowers to Tia. They really were spectacular."

The man's smile widened. "Is that so? And, uh . . . did Miss Witherspoon like them?"

"Like them? Why she adored them. She said they were just about the most beautiful things she'd ever seen," said Dinora.

This seemed to please Mr. Billings immensely. "Well, I'm glad. She really is an extraordinary woman."

"Yeah, she's a peach," Zoë said. "So what'll it be? Carrots? Lettuce? Strawberries?"

"Oh, oh no, no, thank you. I just came by to see if, uh, Miss Witherspoon were, um. Well, I suppose I should be on my way."

"Okay then, bye," said Zoë.

"Goodbye, Mr. Billings," Dinora called amiably. "I'll be sure to tell Tia you dropped by. I'm sure she'd be delighted to know."

"Oh yes, please do. She's a marvelous woman. Positively top grade."

As the elderly man made his way down the street, Seymour chuckled. "Well he's obviously a fan."

"Dinora, would it kill you to just mind your own business for one minute?" Zoë chastised. "Tia can handle things just fine without your meddling."

"What?" Dinora retorted indignantly. "I'm just being sociable. No harm in that."

"Well I say you need to keep your nose out of what doesn't concern you," Zoë warned.

"Like this for instance?" Dinora smiled broadly as she looked over Zoë's shoulder.

"What?"

"*This.*"

It was Eli.

"Hey, Daniel. How's everything selling?"

"So far, so good. Getting a lot of tourists."

"Should be a good summer."

"Ayeh."

Dinora watched the worthless interchange with growing dissatisfaction before ushering the conversation forward. "We're all really looking forward to the dance this Saturday, Eli."

"I'm glad." He looked at Zoë. "I'm looking forward to seeing you there."

Zoë was finding something fascinating about her fingernails.

"Anyway," he stifled a laugh. "See you on Saturday."

Dinora sighed as she watched him leave, then started singing *Isn't It Romantic?* until Zoë shoved a strawberry in her mouth.

11
❧ The Trip ❧

Seymour understood his cousin better than anyone. He also had a wonderful gift for sensing how well the others were faring. Dinora was fine. She was always fine, which Seymour appreciated greatly. That girl could be dropped into a pit of crocodiles and all she'd say would be, "Tea, anyone?" The only concern with Dinora was how much she was bothering Zoë. But this was Zoë's problem and it had plenty of company. Life in China was difficult for her. With her parents traveling so much, she was under the constant rule of her grandmother, who was even more stubborn than Zoë herself.

Seymour had only met Chen Taitai once, but it was a memorable event. He'd been five but that didn't stop her from demanding to know his plans for the future and just how good his calligraphy was. She interrogated him while correcting his pronunciation and posture at the same time. He didn't want to think of what life must be like in the unrelenting iron grip of that formidable woman.

As a result, summers were salvation for Zoë. It was the one time of year when she was free to dress as she liked, eat as she liked, go where she wanted and begin to let down her guard. He knew her first week back on The Island was always a challenge. Transitioning from one world to its complete opposite took a substantial amount of energy. Seymour imagined this must also be true for her return to Nanjing, where she was sure to be greeted with a barrage of criticisms on how much she had let herself slip.

Then there was Daniel. He had been through an emotional wringer. Life had been hard enough for him, growing up without family and coming so late to Tia's. And now he finds a year of his childhood is unaccounted for, he's been lied to about his parents, he has a grandfather who is in jail for murder, and now, at fifteen, he's in possession of a house and a briefcase full of suspicious cash. All of this, but especially the money, was gut-wrenching for him.

Daniel was probably the most honest and honorable person Seymour knew—including adults. Being burdened with something illegal—or even worse, immoral—was tearing the boy up inside. Seymour didn't know how well Daniel usually slept, but he could only assume it was a lot better than how he was sleeping these days. The last few nights, Seymour had been wakened multiple times by Daniel's incoherent shouts. Seymour was seriously worried that his friend would not be able to handle much more of this.

Greta was the most interesting case. She hardly said a word but she noticed everything. And ever since the previous summer's events, she had been especially attuned to Zoë's rollercoaster of feelings. Because Greta wasn't one to share how she was doing (unlike Dinora who blessed all of them with a moment-to-moment update), Seymour was the most concerned about her. When you don't know how to share your feelings and you don't want to draw attention to yourself, there's only one place for those pent up worries to go and that's inward.

Seymour knew it was not his responsibility to take care of the others. Sometimes Zoë teased him for how he made a point of "mothering" everyone. Still, he knew each of them played different roles in the group and this was one of his. He was good at it. He saw the needs and decided on an ideal solution. The idea currently occupying his thoughts would have been worth doing for just Daniel or Zoë or Greta. The fact that all three needed some respite made it a clear choice.

He enlisted help from Tia and Edith. He wanted it to be a surprise for his three friends. He would have asked Dinora but that would have defeated the purpose. Finally, when everything was ready, he went to sleep. It felt like he had just shut his eyes when Edith shook him awake.

"You still want to do this?" she asked gruffly.

Seymour yawned. "It's going to be perfect."

"Okay but be careful and don't do anything stupid."

"I know. Plus, we'll have Daniel and Zoë."

"Yes but you'll also have Greta and Dinora."

Seymour thought about this for a moment and could definitely see Edith's point. It might end up being a wash. "We'll be careful and we'll stay in touch."

"Don't forget. Every twelve hours or we come looking."

"Got it." Seymour was wide awake now as the adrenaline kicked in.

"And keep an eye out along the coastline."

"Edith, you've told me all of this."

"I know, I know. It's not me. I know you kids will be fine. You're tough—all of you. Even the girls."

Seymour knew she was referring specifically to the younger girls. Edith had the utmost respect for Zoë's grit. The older woman continued, "It's Dot. She's worried but she doesn't want you to think she doubts your ability and on and on. It's driving me mad."

"Edith, it'll be fine. It'll be amazing."

"You're right. Okay, I'll be in the truck. We're all loaded up."

"Great. We'll be there in fifteen minutes."

In truth it ended up taking even less than that, in part because the children were accustomed to pre-dawn adventuring and in part because they were intrigued by something that had been planned without their knowledge. They were out of their beds and dressed within minutes. They didn't even pressure Seymour to tell them what was happening. They appreciated the experience and eagerly waited for events to unfold.

When the truck turned toward the docks, Zoë was the first to make a sound. She cried out in delight and looked to Seymour for confirmation. He nodded and she practically flew at him in gratitude.

"*Xie xie, Ximei.*" She embraced her cousin fiercely.

"You're welcome. C'mon. Let's get this boat loaded."

Again within minutes they had loaded *The Prudence* with mysterious bags and boxes. Once the hull was packed, the children waved goodbye to Edith and Zoë started the motor.

"Where to?" she asked.

The sun was just beginning to peek over the horizon, casting a subtle orange light on their shadowy figures.

"Second star on the right," Seymour smiled, pointing at the few remaining stars above them. "And straight on 'til morning."

"Perfect." She hugged him again. "I could do with a little visit to *Neverland.*"

"I think we all could," replied Seymour.

Once they got out into open seas, they wrestled the boom into the wind and battled with the jib. They sailed under a brisk breeze and by the time the sun had fully risen, there was no land in sight.

"So what's the plan?" called Zoë. She was at the tiller now, maneuvering the rudder to capture all possible speed.

Greta was amazed at how quickly they were moving and became anxious when all she could see was water in every direction. Going to Belfast had been one thing. They had traveled from The Island to the mainland, never leaving the confines of the bay. This was different. Soon the waters were darker, the waves more violent and Greta got nauseous just at the thought of what might be lurking beneath them. She looked up to see Zoë's beaming face and carefree smile. *She needs this*, Greta thought. She looked at Daniel who, for the first time in a week, appeared as if he wasn't carrying the weight of the world on his shoulders. *He needs this too. Perhaps we all do. I wonder how Seymour knew.* She turned and met his eyes. In silent communication of praise and appreciation, she nodded confidently at him. "Yeah," she called. "What is the plan?"

Seymour gathered them together and instructed Zoë and Daniel to lower the sails. Once they did, the boat slowed until it just bobbed happily in waters that were calmer and bluer.

"We need to unpack and get organized. But first," Seymour turned to Dinora, "will you grab the wicker basket on top of those boxes?"

She retrieved it and inside was a picnic breakfast, complete with two thermoses of hot coffee and cocoa.

"Breakfast!" proclaimed Seymour and they all proceeded to tuck in.

"When do we have to be back?" asked Zoë, after relishing some *pan de dulce* dipped in hot chocolate.

"Not until tomorrow afternoon, but—" Seymour took a sip of his coffee. "Edith said if this trip goes well, she'd help convince Tia to let us take a longer one.

The Trip

There was a silence as the children enjoyed their breakfast and the natural beauty around them, and contemplated what a week at sea might be like.

"The first thing to decide is where to go," said Seymour.

"We could sail up to Newfoundland," suggested Zoë.

"It's too far. Plus we'd be in Canadian waters so we'd need our papers," said Daniel. He was holding a plastic-covered map. He turned it so they could see. "Here," he said. "There's a string of uninhabited islands about forty knots southeast of here. Why don't we sail there and camp out on one of them?"

"I love it!" Zoë declared and the others agreed. As Dinora and Greta cleaned up, the stronger and more experienced children worked to once again raise the mainsail in the thick wind. When it was finally secured, the boat, which had started pulling westward as the sail was being raised, lurched ahead and was off. This time Daniel took the rudder and gradually the boat swung a wide arc until they were facing the right direction.

"Greta? How'd you like to help me unpack and get organized down below?" asked Seymour.

Again Greta was impressed with how in tune Seymour was with her wishes. Taking a break from the limitless ocean was just what she needed, especially with a stomach full of food. Together they sifted through the supplies and found places for everything. In the small boat, it was like fitting together puzzle pieces but eventually, everything had a home and there was still enough room for all of them to sleep, but only just.

"It'll definitely be roomier camping out," Seymour said as he and Greta surveyed their work.

"And less nautical," she added and Seymour laughed.

When they joined the others, Daniel was teaching Dinora how to sail. "So these lines are called 'jib sheets'. They're used to control the trim of the jib."

"Trim of the jib! I love that! Trim of the jib, trim of the jib, trim of the—oh! Hi, Greta!" Dinora welcomed exuberantly. "Guess what these are called?" She didn't give time for an answer. "The trim of the jib!" She fell into a fit of giggles. Eventually she was laughing so hard that she slipped and fell. This made her laugh even more and the others couldn't help but join in.

All except Zoë, but before she could do more than roll her eyes, Seymour was there to distract her with a compass and a question.

They sailed until early afternoon when Dinora cried, "Land ho, mateys!"

They looked, and indeed, off in the distance was a speck of grey. An hour later it had grown into a tiny island. And since it was uninhabited and utterly insignificant there were no buoys posted to mark the rocks. Tectonic shifting hundreds of millions of years earlier had created an aquatic terrain that could destroy a boat in minutes. Zoë, showing the prudence Tia had wished for her, slowed the boat well short of the shore. With the boys helping, she quickly lowered the sail and suddenly the boat lost its momentum and became as docile as a rubber ducky in a bathtub.

"Let's drop anchor here," said Zoë. "I don't want to risk getting any closer."

"Good thing," Daniel said. "Look there." He pointed to a sharp rock which barely met the surface of the water. The tip ducked and surged as the waves danced around it, making it virtually indistinguishable from a wave itself. It was about ten meters from their prow.

"Jeepers!" Dinora cried. "Zoë, that was a close one."

"Daniel, do you think the dinghy will make it?" Seymour asked.

"We'll need to go slowly," he assessed. "And probably it'll take at least three trips, maybe four to get all of us and the supplies ashore. We can take an extra oar and use that to feel for anything. Even so, we may have to swim the last bit."

"Swim?" Greta gulped.

"You'll be fine, Greta," said Seymour. "It won't be that far—half a swimming pool at most."

"Swimming pool," she echoed, repeating this silently as the others put their plan into action.

Daniel started the motor and backed the boat farther away to make sure they were safe before dropping anchor. As Seymour and Zoë loosed the dinghy, they hammered out the final details on the supplies.

"It's supposed to be a good night. Let's just take sleeping bags and leave the tents here," Seymour finished. "That'll save a trip."

Seymour, Daniel and Dinora were the first to go.

Dinora helped by keeping an eye out for rocks as if she were playing a preschooler's game. "No rock . . . no rock . . . no rock . . . ROCK!"

"Good grief," Zoë groaned, as she and Greta watched the others navigate their way to the tiny island.

It was maybe a kilometer in diameter, making it roughly the size of a large estate with extensive grounds. For an island however, this was miniscule and Greta was surprised it had even made it onto the map.

It took what was left of the afternoon to unload everything and set up camp. While the others made a trip to shore, Seymour stayed on the sailboat to radio an update to Edith and set out his fishing line. Soon he felt a tug and by the time they returned, he'd caught dinner.

"Be sure to gut them here," Zoë advised. "It'll attract birds if we do it on land."

Once they were all ashore, they were delegated to their various tasks. Zoë dug a shallow pit, lined it with rocks and started the fire. Greta and Dinora used branches to clear a place where they could lay down their ancient canvas tarpaulin. And although it was only a one-person job, Seymour accompanied Daniel, who ventured with a hatchet toward a copse of pine trees. They worked in contemplative silence, hacking a wind-felled tree into more manageable pieces.

After a while Seymour broached the subject that still hovered over all of them. "If he were my grandfather, I'd want to meet him."

"Has your grandfather murdered anyone recently?"

Seymour returned to silence.

A few minutes later, Daniel set down the hatchet. "I'm sorry. I shouldn't have said that."

"Forget about it."

"I wish I could. I wish I could forget this whole blasted thing. The box, the money—"

"Daniel, you owe it to yourself. He's your only family. Maybe there's more to the story."

"There is more. Greta told me. He was a scientist, a doctor—if you can believe that—and he killed his partner."

"Did the article say why?"

"Nothing, and she couldn't find anything else except the one where he was sentenced."

"I don't know what to say. I can't even imagine what it must be like to lose your family and then discover . . . this." Seymour sighed. "Just think about it though, okay?"

Daniel said something indistinguishable and the boys returned to their task. After gathering enough wood to last more than one night, they followed the scent of roasting fish and made their way back to camp.

Dinner was delicious. The fish, which Zoë had speared and set on a crudely-fashioned rotisserie, were so delectable the children burned the tips of their fingers in their eagerness to sample another morsel of the revolving food. After dinner they sat around the fire telling ghost stories and reminiscing about childhood antics well into the night. The moon and stars directly above them shone so brightly, it felt as though one could almost reach out and pluck them from the sky. The children banked the fire and nestled into their sleeping bags.

The Trip

For three of them, it was the first peaceful night they'd had since summer had begun.

12

✤ The Bet ✤

The restful mood remained through the next morning. The children lingered over breakfast before packing up and returning their belongings to the boat. After delivering the final load, they decided to thoroughly explore the island, which, even with great precision, took less than an hour to survey. Most exciting was a clearing on the north end which played host to a clump of perfectly arranged pines.

"We could build a tree house here!" Dinora exclaimed. "Wouldn't that be wonderful? Just like in *Swiss Family Robinson*."

Although it wasn't feasible at the moment, they all enjoyed mapping out how it might be designed, complete with a second floor.

"Ow!" Dinora yelped.

"You okay?" asked Seymour.

"I guess. I keep stubbing my toe on these iron roots."

"Well, try to be more careful."

"What a helpful suggestion, Seymour. Ever consider writing your own advice column?" Zoë teased.

The Bet

"Yeah, I have, Zo. I thought I'd call it *How to Tolerate Sarcastic Cousins.*"

She punched him playfully and they raced each other back to the shore. Soon they were all aboard *The Prudence* and navigating away from the island to raise the sail. The sun was blazing and it didn't take long for the children to begin sweltering in the heat.

"Let's stop for a swim!" Seymour shouted. Once again the oldest children worked to warp *The Prudence* into the breeze. This was the wonderful thing about Friendship Sloops. The two little headsails worked in concert with the larger mainsail and moments after luffing, the boat was steady. Seymour was the first in. He tore off his tee shirt, kicked off his sneakers and dove neatly into the ocean. Greta knew he could stay under for a long time but even so, she had to avert her eyes. When she finally heard his voice she looked and saw him off in the distance.

"It's great!" he yelled back. One by one the others joined him—except for Greta, who found it was all she could do to stay on deck and pray the boat could handle itself. Frolicking in the open sea without anyone else around was an incredible experience and when they came aboard for lunch, Greta noted that all of them were in best form. Even Zoë.

Unfortunately, this did not last for very long.

Zoë was relishing the tranquility of the ocean when Dinora once again started laughing about "the trim of the jib".

"Dinora, do you have to prattle on about absolutely everything? Did you ever think that maybe some of us might like a little peace and quiet?"

Dinora seemed to consider this for the first time.

"I bet you couldn't keep quiet if you tried. I bet you couldn't refrain from talking for a single hour."

"And what if I did?" Dinora asked, her good spirits unfettered by Zoë's comment.

"Huh?"

"What if I did? You said, 'I bet' and I say, 'what if'."

"You know what Dinora? I am so sure you will not be able to keep your mouth shut for ten minutes, let alone an hour, that you can ask for anything at all."

"Anything?"

"Anything."

"Okay then." She smiled broadly. "If I win, you have to go to the dance tonight."

"Are you crazy?"

"You did say 'anything', Zoë," Seymour called from the stern, reminding her that this was not a private conversation.

"But—never mind. It won't even matter." She turned to shake Dinora's hand. "Deal. You keep quiet for an hour and I go to the dance. You don't and I won't. Now who's got a watch?"

Seymour passed his watch to Greta, the agreed-upon judge, who made a note of the time. Once started, Dinora shut her mouth, walked primly to the other end of the boat, turned to stare at the ocean and didn't say a single word.

An hour later, three surprised children and one stunned girl had to admit that Dinora had accomplished the unthinkable.

"Hooray!" she cried when her victory was declared and acknowledged. "Oh, Zoë, it's going to be so much fun. There will be music and dancing and girls in beautiful dresses and boys and . . . *Eli*. Oh, I'm so excited you're coming. Hooray, hooray, hooray! For a second there I didn't think I was going to be able to do it. It was a lot more difficult than I thought. But then I just kept telling myself—'Self, think of Zoë. Think of how much fun she'll have at the dance. Think of the look on Eli's face when she walks through that door.' And that got me through." Dinora replenished her lungs. "Although I did have to repeat the conversation many, many times. But it was worth it." She hugged Zoë tightly, who was still standing there, dumbfounded. Greta wasn't sure if this was because of the dance or Dinora's amazing feat of silence. "Hooray, hooray, hoo—"

"Double or nothing," said Zoë.

"—ray? Huh?"

"Double or nothing. We do it again. You go for another hour. If you can't do it, I don't have to go to the dance and if you can—"

"Zoë, that's not fair," Seymour butted in.

"What's not fair about it? It's a perfectly valid bet."

"She won, Zo. Fair and—"

"I can do it, Seymour," Dinora insisted.

"Not likely," Zoë scoffed.

"She did it once," Seymour reminded her, earning a glare.

"I get to dress you," Dinora blurted.

"What?"

"That's how it works, right? If I don't do it, you don't have to go to the dance, but if I do do it." Dinora giggled. "Do-do."

Zoë looked to the heavens, silently imploring the fates to free her from such immaturity.

"If I *do* do it," Dinora paused to regain her composure, "then you have to do something I want. Right?"

"Yes," Zoë consented reluctantly.

Dinora paused again but this time it was for effect. "Then I choose dressing you. If I don't talk for another hour, then you have to wear what I say."

"Hah!" Zoë honked. "No way, no how!"

"You did say she wouldn't be able to do it. So what does it matter what she wants." Seymour was enjoying this.

"Well even a broken clock is right twice a day—it could happen again."

"Then why bet her?"

"Because I don't want to go," whined Zoë.

"It's a dance, Zoë. It's not jail—oh, sorry, Danny," Dinora apologized but he was oblivious.

"Why do you even care?" Zoë accused.

"Because I care about you and it'll be fun."

"Okay, fine. But if you make so much as a peep, then . . ." Zoë left the rest unfinished.

"No peeping from me." She smiled at Greta. "Peep," she whispered, before, once again nodding to Zoë, turning starboard and commencing her end of the bargain.

By the time they returned home, Dinora had not only won the right to dress Zoë but now the girl had to dance with the Eaton boy as well.

"What if he doesn't ask me?"

"He'll ask," they all said in unison, even Daniel.

"Hmph."

"And don't try to get out of it by avoiding him all night," cautioned her cousin between fits of laughter.

"I know how it works, Seymour," snapped Zoë. "I don't renege on my bets."

"What about the time you told Sally LeGro you'd buy her a dog if she gave you her lollipop?"

"We were three."

"True, but I'm not sure if a leopard ever really changes her spots."

"Watch out for the boom," Zoë called, a little too late. It swung wide and barely missed knocking Seymour into the water.

"Play nice, Zoë," he called back, smiling in sheer amusement.

13

➢ The Dance ⤎

When they got closer to The Island, Seymour radioed ahead to notify Edith. She was waiting for them on the dock and even she noticed a world of difference in their spirits.

"Sometimes getting away can heal all sorts of wounds," she told Seymour before noticing Dinora's smug smile and lack of chattering. "What's wrong with the girl?"

"Long story but you're just in time for the climax."

"Hmph."

When they arrived at Tia's the children soaked in bathtubs, rested and ate a quick supper. Afterward, two of the girls (one with delight and the other with dread) commenced their ordeal. Things did get dicey as Dinora and Zoë had a heated conversation about whether or not "makeup" was considered part of a girl's "outfit" but eventually the artist acquiesced and the girls descended the stairs.

Dinora came first in yellow chiffon. Seymour let out a wolf whistle and she fanned herself in mock modesty before inspecting their attire. The boys were both in dress pants, collared shirts, short jackets and ties. "You don't look too shabby yourself, sailors," she said in her best Mae West imitation.

"And Zoë?" Seymour called.

"Oh, Zo-ee," Dinora cooed. "Your public awaits."

There was some grumbling upstairs, which Greta suspected contained more than a few words not used in church, before Zoë stomped down and turned the corner to face the firing squad.

Greta and the boys stood in awe.

"Nice threads," remarked Seymour, clearly impressed with Dinora's handiwork.

"Dinora, she's beautiful," Daniel too complimented the artist. This seemed fitting since what they saw before them was clearly none of Zoë's doing. Furthermore, the way she stood stoically before them made her look as if she actually were in a painting. The image was breathtaking. Dinora had found a scarlet taffeta dress that fit Zoë as if made for her. She wasn't wearing any makeup and Greta thought she didn't need it. Her face was unequivocally unique and flawless, with lips naturally a deep pink color and thick lashes framing eyes of such a light brown they almost seemed amber. To top it all off, Dinora had pinned Zoë's thick black hair in intricate swirls, adorned with small red roses from Tia's garden.

A bizarre notion entered Greta's mind. There was Twist 'n' Turn Barbie and Malibu Barbie. *Now there's Life-Size Barbie!* Greta thought even Dinora's expression looked like the one on the face of the delighted girl in the commercials.

"If you all are quite finished gawking, I have a dance to attend and I don't want to be late," said Zoë in feigned haughtiness and resigned humor.

Dinora and the boys whooped in delight and they all headed out.

Greta had opted not to go. She liked the idea of a quiet evening at home and Tia had agreed to help her with one of the items from her O.G.D. list. With the others gone, this would be the perfect night for it. She waved goodbye to her friends, who seemed ready to embrace an enjoyable evening. Even Zoë. Reentering the kitchen, Greta noticed a new spectacular bouquet of flowers and a card on the counter. Edith was sitting at the large oak table sipping tea and reading an old book.

Tia set out a plate of raspberry tarts. "Oh Edith, darling, he's harmless. Absolutely harmless," Tia assured, sampling the confection before placing the flowers into a gigantic porcelain pitcher.

Edith had a bemused expression on her face. She didn't even look up from her book as she responded, "You don't need to tell me, Dot."

When they arrived at the grange, Eli was standing outside the door. He ambled toward the truck and opened the passenger side door for Dinora, who accepted his hand and hopped out. Zoë too let Eli take her hand but with a moment of obvious hesitation.

"I'm actually a little surprised you came," he said. They were trailing the others, who had entered the hall, a world of boisterous fiddling and stomping. Community members, young and old, had gathered from across The Island. "When I invited you, you didn't seem terribly interested." A smile played on his face.

"Picked up on that, did you?"

He laughed. "So what changed your mind? Was it my charming personality? The beautiful evening?" He motioned to her outfit. "A chance to show off your new frock?"

"I lost a bet."

"Oh." He laughed heartily. They had entered the large room with open-beamed ceilings, a stage for the band on one end and tables with punch and dessert on the other. "I see. Well, if you don't want to dance, I certainly don't want to force you."

Zoë looked around to see if Dinora was watching. The younger girl was staring directly at her, a huge grin plastered across her face.

"We're already here," said Zoë. "We might as well."

"I guess I've heard worse reasons," said Eli, guiding her toward the dance floor.

The previous song had just ended and flushed-faced dancers were making their way to the edges of the room to catch their breath, quench their thirst and enjoy some conversation. They were quickly replaced with the next round of foursomes. Zoë noticed Seymour hadn't wasted any time. He was paired up with a redheaded girl at the far end of the room. Zoë also noticed Dinora's bright yellow dress as she and Daniel made their way to another group. Eli led her and they joined a couple she'd come to know very well over the years.

"Why, Zoë Chen, as I live and breathe. You look about as lovely as an angel," the older woman cooed.

"Meribah, don't you embarrass the girl in front of her beau," Doctor Ingraham scolded, not sensing his comment was just as humiliating.

But Zoë didn't have the opportunity to respond. The band had struck up again and before she knew it, her *quadrille* was in full motion. Even by modern standards, the Ingrahams were energetic and enthusiastic dancers. As Zoë found herself swung and twirled, she experienced a freedom she'd only felt in one other place.

"Having fun?" Eli asked her. They were linking arms and following the caller's elaborate footwork instructions, which Zoë was rapidly remembering from her childhood. "Because you kind of look like you're having fun."

"It's like sailing," she said, rewarding him with a heartfelt smile. "Thank you."

"My pleasure," he beamed back. "Really."

The music stopped and another girl swooped in between them. "Eli, you have to dance with me," she pouted. "There's no one else here but old men. No offense, Doctor Ingraham."

The elderly physician chuckled knowingly. "None taken, Ivy."

Zoë turned around to find another partner. This dancing business had an addictive allure. She saw Daniel and rushed toward him. "Daniel, it's wonderful!"

He laughed. "I know!" And because he was a gentleman and a friend, he refrained from reminding her that Dinora had predicted just that, repeatedly.

The music started again, and as she began the steps more confidently, she noticed someone staring at her from across the room. He was underneath the lower ceiling that supported the second floor balcony, where the other half of the town was visiting, eating, watching the dancers and gossiping. Zoë couldn't see his face clearly but she had no doubt about the object of his attention.

Hour after hour passed and Zoë only stopped when one boy or another brought her punch. Then she was back in the swing and having the time of her life. But she wasn't so entranced as to miss it when, again, the man was staring right at her. It was unnerving. Still, she tried to put it out of her mind as her dance with Daniel ended and the next one began. This time she paired up with Seymour, who himself had been quite popular throughout the evening.

Zoë saw fit to point this out. "Well you certainly seem to be having a nice time."

"What can I say?" He spoke loudly, so as to be heard over the raucous music. "I'm a sociable person."

They danced until the band quit and everyone was exhausted.

Zoë looked around but didn't see the man anywhere. "There was a guy watching us earlier," she told the others.

"You're so vain, Zo," Seymour teased. "Just because you're the belle of the ball and a model to boot doesn't mean—"

"Shut up, Seymour! That's not true!"

"Okay, okay. I'm sorry. I was just joking."

"Don't say that. You know how I feel about that. You know how much I hate doing it. It's my only option and now I can't even . . ."

"Can't what?"

Zoë was struggling to contain her feelings. "Forget about it," she said.

"What did he look like?" asked Daniel.

Zoë was relieved to talk about something else. "I didn't see too well. He was older—had white hair—tall, broad shoulders. Kind of distinguished looking—like an old movie star."

"And he was staring at you," swooned Dinora. "Maybe you reminded him of a young Carole Lombard."

"I didn't say *staring*. I said *watching*. And I didn't say *me*, I said *us*. Jeez, don't any of you listen?"

"Is he here now?" Daniel asked.

"No, but . . . I don't know. It was probably nothing."

"Zoë?" Dinora sidled up to her and put an arm around her waist. "Did you have a simply marvelous time?"

"What? Oh. Yes, Dinora," she said. "I had a great time."

The two boys cleared their throats simultaneously.

"Thank you," she added.

"You're most welcome!"

14

❧ The Past ❧

Sleeping in would have been wonderful but Saturday was Saturday and that meant the market. So the children dragged themselves out of bed, grabbed a muffin, loaded the truck and drove into town. They set up their stall nearly an hour late and yet it was just in time. A good many of the town's gardeners had been at the dance the night before and subsequently the market itself was having a slow start. There were the loyal customers and a slew of tourists but they all came early so by ten o'clock the ennui of a lazy Saturday morning had settled in. It didn't last long though, as a series of very eventful visitations was about to ensue.

The first to call was Eli Eaton, who wanted to make certain they'd enjoyed the dance. After they assured him this was most definitely the case, he extended a second invitation to the church picnic the very next afternoon. To the astonishment of all, it was Dinora who declined.

"We'd love to, Eli, but we have plans. I certainly hope to find something else we can do together though, *soon*. It's such a pleasure spending time with nice people."

He laughed. "Okay then. Some other time."

The rest of the morning trickled by and at noon the children decided to pack up and salvage what portion of the day they could. Just as they began, their second visitor arrived. It was a besotted Mr. Billings, who again inquired after Tia and again was disappointed not to find her there at the moment. He asked if she had enjoyed the flowers and Dinora told him that all eight bouquets had been very well received.

"I would shift gears though, Mr. Billings," Dinora advised. "Flowers will only get you so far. You might consider chocolates next. I know that Tia is especially fond of Belgian truffles. Preferably, dark chocolate."

Mr. Billings thanked her profusely for the tip and headed straight for *The Bonbon Shop*, which Dinora had recommended quite highly.

As the man left, Seymour wondered aloud, "That's strange. Correct me if I'm wrong but aren't dark chocolate Belgian truffles *your* favorite, Dinora?"

"And what if they are? We both happen to like them, thank you very much. They're quite tasty. Besides, so many flowers make the house feel like a funeral parlor."

"Speaking of funerals," Daniel said, nodding toward a very intent young woman marching officiously their way.

Seymour started humming the theme song for the Wicked Witch of the West from *The Wizard of Oz*.

"Oh Seymour, honestly," scolded Dinora. "She can't be that bad."

"Good morning," Ivy droned contemptuously, conveying that she hoped, in fact, it *wasn't* a good morning and that, if it was, she had every intention of remedying that soon enough.

"Uh, Zoë, I think we're going to let you handle this one," said Seymour, quickly stepping out of Ivy's way. The others followed in quick succession.

"Why me?" she asked but they were already out of the stall, if not earshot.

"Listen up, you." Ivy went on the offensive.

Zoë looked around and could only deduce this obnoxious girl must be speaking to her.

"Yes, you," confirmed Ivy. "Let me get right to the point. Eli is my boyfriend. Get it? *Mine.* If you so much as look at him again, I'm going to make you regret you ever came to this island. Do you *understand* that?"

Zoë just stared at her. "Let me get this straight." She started to laugh. "You're threatening me? About a boy?" She laughed even harder. "Listen, believe me—*believe me*—you have nothing to worry about. That boy is probably the last thing on my mind. I *wish* my life was that simple."

This apparently was not one of the responses for which Ivy was prepared. She stammered a moment before announcing haughtily, "Very well then. I'm glad we've reached an understanding."

"I guess," answered Zoë but Ivy had already huffed, turned and was now parading down Main Street.

Then Zoë saw him—the man from the dance. She didn't recognize the face; it had been too shadowed. But the stance was clearly familiar—as if he owned the block. He was dressed in a linen summer suit, beige in color but probably called something fancier in the expensive store where he'd purchased it, or had it tailored.

He walked right up to her. "Excuse me, miss. I'm looking for Daniel Sutton. I believe he was here with you this morning?"

"Daniel?" Zoë coughed, looking as perplexed as Ivy had moments earlier.

Upon hearing his name, Daniel emerged from behind the truck. "I'm Daniel Sutton," he said cautiously.

The man reached out his hand. It was tanned, along with his face, as if he wintered in Florida or the Bahamas. His teeth were exceptionally white. "How do you do, Daniel? I'm Dr. George Huntington. I'm a dear friend of your grandfather's. I was hoping we could talk for a bit. Maybe I could take you to lunch?"

Daniel hesitated.

"Of course, your friends are welcome too, if you like." He somehow managed to indicate all of them without taking his piercing blue eyes off Daniel.

"You're a friend of his?"

Dr. Huntington nodded.

"Then you know—"

"That he was imprisoned for a crime he didn't commit? Yes, I know."

Daniel was silent.

"Danny, it really is a long story." He looked disparagingly at their stall. "This isn't the best . . . *place* . . . for it. Will you come?"

Daniel turned to the others, whose expressions indicated it was his decision to make. "Okay," he said. "We'll come."

"Wonderful," Dr. Huntington's voice warmed. "Shall we head over to *Mandy's*? I haven't eaten one of her cheeseburgers in ages."

"Capital idea!" said Dinora, linking her arm in his and introducing everyone in one breath.

Once inside the diner, Dr. Huntington directed them to a corner table, which afforded a little privacy. He made a point of sitting directly across from Daniel. The waitress came over immediately but before she could pass out the menus, Dr. Huntington ordered, "Cheeseburgers, fries and cherry cokes all around."

"Yes, sir," she said, with what looked like a slight curtsy.

"Danny, I'm assuming it would be helpful if I just started at the beginning?" asked Dr. Huntington.

"Sure. That's fine, I guess."

"Let's see, well, your grandfather and I were the best of friends in high school—the three of us were. Lionel too. Inseparable. You wouldn't find one of us without the other two being right there alongside." He smiled wistfully at the memory. "After we graduated, we all went to Dartmouth and then on to Harvard for medical school. At one time we had dreamed about opening a practice together in Boston but the timing never worked out. For one thing, your grandfather wanted to continue his research work. He was an amazing scientist, Danny." Dr. Huntington paused to look intently at Daniel.

"Uh, thank you, sir," he said in obvious discomfort.

Dr. Huntington smiled before continuing, "Soon we had our own families, but we always stayed close." A pained expression came across his face. He looked down to compose himself, then reached to pat Daniel's hand. "Danny, they were like brothers to me. It kills me to think of what happened—to both of them."

The waitress brought their food and the children began eating as they listened to the story unfold.

"Then the army needed doctors. It was your grandfather who enlisted first. He was always thinking of others. I admit I was the selfish one. I couldn't bear to leave my wife and daughters. But our country needed us, and soon Lionel and I joined up as well." He paused again as he seemed to struggle with memories of war.

"After that, I got a job at a pharmaceutical company, right over in Belfast. I insisted they take your grandfather and Lionel too. Your grandfather had a brilliant mind, Danny—an incredible mind. Lionel was exceptional but it was your grandfather who . . . who made great strides in the field. I daresay, we made quite a bit of money off him." He smiled. "We were all so happy in those days. Simpler times, I suppose. We led our lives, raised our kids. Felicia, your mother, she was a beautiful girl. It was a shame to lose her." He scrutinized Daniel. "You don't favor her though. No, you are the spitting image of your grandfather, even carrying his name."

"You said you thought my grandfather was falsely imprisoned."

Dr. Huntington smiled. "You're quick like your grandfather, too. Yes, I'm sure he didn't kill Lionel. Like I said, they were so close, more than partners. Daniel wouldn't have hurt him. Couldn't have hurt him, or anyone for that matter. He was kindness incarnate, that man."

"Was?" asked Zoë suspiciously.

Dr. Huntington eyed her coldly. "And is still, to be sure. Yes. I was the only one who stood by him. There's simply no way he could have done it—no matter what evidence they had against him. He loved Lionel like a brother, but there was no way to prove it." He reached for Daniel's hand again. "I even asked the court to give me custody of you, Danny. Your grandfather begged me to take you and I promised him I'd try. I did, but the paperwork wasn't in place and even though I thought of you as family, the court didn't."

Daniel seemed to consider this. "How'd you find me?"

"Hmm?" Dr. Huntington took a sip of his coke.

"I said, how'd you find me?"

"You know, it was the darndest thing. I lost track of you after the trial. The state took you and placed you somewhere."

"*The Brewster Boys Home*," said Daniel.

"I'm sorry about that, Danny. That's no way for a boy to grow up. And now what's it been? Ten years?"

Daniel nodded.

"Ten years. And it just so happened last week I was in Boston giving a talk to a group of interns. Craziest thing—I must have mentioned being from The Island. Then afterward, a young Latin fellow—"

"Latino," corrected Zoë, with poorly concealed contempt.

"Zoë, don't be rude," admonished Seymour.

"That's all right, young man. Some countries don't teach children to respect their elders." The older man didn't bother to look at her. "She may not know any better."

"Please continue, Dr. Huntington," said Daniel.

"Yes, well, anyway, this particular intern mentioned he used to summer here."

"That's my brother!" Dinora shouted.

"You don't say?" He gave her a brilliant smile. "Well, it sure is a small world. So we got to talking and he mentioned your name. I couldn't believe my luck. Then I came to the dance last night and saw you there."

"You see, Zoë?" said Dinora. "He wasn't staring at *you*, he was staring at *Danny*! Ouch!" Dinora looked hurt and confused. Seymour on the other hand didn't look at all confused. He whispered something to Zoë in Mandarin and she growled her reply.

"And the rest you know," finished Dr. Huntington, reaching into the breast pocket of his suit.

"Yes," agreed Daniel.

"Listen, Danny. I know this must be pretty overwhelming and that's perfectly understandable." He pulled out a thin leather wallet. "Let me leave you and your friends to enjoy your lunch and I'll be on my way." He withdrew a bill large enough to cover a meal twice as big, and set it next to the food he'd never touched.

Greta noticed Daniel too hadn't eaten.

Dr. Huntington removed a crisp white card with a blue "H" on it. "This has all of my information, Danny. If you need anything—anything at all—you let me know. If I can help, I will. I promise you." He stood up, started to leave, but then turned back to face them.

"A thought just occurred to me. Danny, did your grandfather leave anything for you?"

Daniel looked confused. "Like what?"

"Anything that might help prove his innocence?"

"I didn't even know he existed until a few days ago."

Dr. Huntington sighed. "I suppose that would have been too easy. If you think of anything, son, let me know. I'd be honored to help. I only wish I could have done more." This time when he left, he kept walking.

"What a piece of work," groaned Zoë. "Can you believe him?" She lowered her voice and said with suave intensity, "Son, I only wish I could have done more."

The others stared at her.

"What?"

No one said anything.

"You've got to be kidding me. None of you saw through that clown?"

"Zoë," said Seymour. "He was only trying to help."

She stared at him, then turned away to sulk.

"Danny, what do you think," asked Dinora.

Daniel set the card on the table.

DR. GEORGE T. HUNTINGTON
VICE PRESIDENT OF RESEARCH & DEVELOPMENT
HAVERHILL CHEMICALS
32 BROADWAY AVENUE
ROCKLAND, MAINE

"I want to meet him," he said, looking at each of them in turn. "I want to meet my grandfather."

"I'm so relieved," Dinora sighed heavily.

"Why's that?"

"Because I made an appointment for tomorrow morning."

15

❧ The Jail ❧

They only had to break the law a little. The children tried to think of another way but in the end, their choice was either to enlist Tia's help or drive the truck off The Island without a license. Although Daniel abhorred either idea, his vehement opposition to anyone else knowing about his grandfather tipped the scale. Reluctantly, he agreed. As they prepared, Greta silently noted the irony of breaking the law in order to visit someone in jail.

Nearing the ferry, Daniel pulled the truck over and swapped places with Seymour who, with spurts and starts, finally managed to get to the ferry terminal and onto the boat. Since Daniel looked fifteen, but Seymour, at over 80 centimeters, looked at least eighteen, the lady who sold them their ticket paid little notice and let them pass.

Getting aboard the ferry had been their first dilemma. Their second had been money. On The Island everyone accepted credit. During the summer, Tia would get a regular bill from the gas station or grocery store and a significant one from the ice cream parlor and she would pay them. Away from The Island, Tia was suddenly transformed from an institution to an address. Cash was needed on the mainland. None of them had much since they rarely needed it. Daniel, on the other hand, had a briefcase full of it.

Even with the others insisting it wasn't stealing, Daniel only agreed to take thirty dollars. It was something he could repay on Monday from the money in his own bank account. The proceeds from the market went to him but Tia didn't like him spending it. She referred to it as his college fund and although he doubted he'd ever make it there, he respected her too much to argue.

Once the ferry departed, the boys swapped places again. There was a bus depot a few miles from the ferry and Daniel only needed to be able to get that far. They had decided the night before it wasn't worth trying to drive to Bangor. First of all, Daniel had no experience driving more than sixty kilometers an hour. Second, it was against the law and none of them was interested in tempting fate. The third and final reason was the most convincing. They had already stretched Tia's trust by asking to skip church just this once so they could go hiking on the other side of The Island. It would shatter her trust if they got caught driving to Bangor without license *or* permission.

The timing worked out just as Seymour had planned. They bought five roundtrip tickets to Bangor and boarded the half-full bus, which left minutes later. It was a two-hour ride and Daniel didn't speak for any of it. Dinora made small talk with Greta, who shared her seat. Zoë slept and Seymour contemplated their clues. Something didn't make sense. The papers were useless— a movie stub and ferry schedule? And even though he'd never met Daniel's grandfather, he just couldn't picture him as a cold-blooded killer. Maybe Dr. Huntington was right and the man was innocent. There had to be more to the story.

Once in Bangor, they took a taxi to a small café where the others would wait. Daniel insisted on being alone for his visit to the Maine State Penitentiary.

"We'll be right here waiting for you, Danny," said Dinora. "You're sure you don't want us to come?"

"I'm fine. Thanks," he replied tersely, before closing the taxi door.

The children found a table, ordered iced tea and prepared to wait for an indefinite amount of time.

"I think someone's tailing us," Zoë said under her breath.

"Oh, not again," complained Seymour.

"What do you mean 'oh, not again'?" she accused. "Wasn't I right about your pal George?"

"I think he prefers 'Dr. Huntington'," said Dinora.

"Like I care. Look, believe me or don't, but it's true."

"Fine," Seymour humored her. "Who's *tailing* us?"

"Don't all look at once but it's the tall man in the black suit sitting by the front door."

They all turned to look.

"What did I just say?" Zoë whispered violently.

"Sorry," mouthed Dinora, before explaining. "I assumed we were looking alphabetically." She pointed out the order.

It clearly took considerable effort for Zoë not to be sidetracked by this remark. "Anyway, he was on the bus too. Doesn't that seem strange?"

"Frightfully," deadpanned Seymour.

"*And* he keeps eyeballing us," said Zoë and as Dinora opened her mouth she reiterated, "I said *us*, Dinora. Not *me*. *Us*."

"Why do you have to be so suspicious, Zoë?" Seymour reprimanded. "First Dr. Huntington, now this poor fellow. So what if the guy was on our bus? It's a free country."

Zoë was clearly injured by this last comment and proceeded to stew in silence as the others passed the remaining time discussing what Daniel must be doing at this exact moment.

The kilometer to the jail took the longest five minutes of his life and was followed immediately by 50 minutes of steps, stages and protocols. These flew by in no time. Now Daniel was sitting in a square grey cement block room with a smattering of tables and chairs: the visiting room. And it looked to Daniel as if not many people were receiving visitors these days. He watched as the door at the far end of the room opened.

For someone who had been a schoolmate of George Huntington's, the man who entered could not have been less like him. Whereas Dr. Huntington was tall and muscular, this man was hunched and atrophied. Whereas one was tanned and perfectly groomed, the other was pale and looked as if he rarely bathed. And whereas one was animated and charming, the other seemed vacant and indifferent.

A heavyset guard gently guided the older man to the table where Daniel sat. "Mr. Sutton," he said at an elevated volume. "Sir, you sit right here." He motioned to the chair, and although the man spoke slowly and loudly, Daniel got the impression he could have yelled and it wouldn't have mattered. The prisoner was lost in another world and not at all the man Daniel had expected to meet.

"Mr. Sutton, this here's your grandson," the guard continued.

"Grandson?" The voice was hoarse and choppy.

"Yes, sir. Your grandson."

"Oh."

Daniel didn't know what to say to that. He didn't know what to say at all.

"Sorry, kid," the kind guard said. "This may be as good as it gets."

"What's wrong with him?" Daniel asked.

"He's old, I guess. I've been here almost five years and he's been like this the whole time. Sometimes he has fits—starts screaming and yelling nonsense—but most days . . . most days he's like this."

"Can I talk to him? Will he understand me?"

"You can try. Every once in a while I see something in his eyes, makes me think he gets it but I couldn't say for sure."

"Melon," the old man creaked.

"What's that, old-timer?"

"My grandson. His name is 'Melon'."

"No, sir. This *here's* your grandson. His name is Daniel—just like you, sir."

The old man grunted a response.

"I'll leave you two to visit," said the guard.

"Melon, Melon, Melon," he mumbled. Then his head jerked up so quickly it scared Daniel. Their eyes locked. "Flowers!" he shouted. "Flowers! Flowers! Flowers!" He sounded like a deranged parrot.

"Shut up, you." Now it was a different guard who approached, also young, but who clearly spent all his spare time lifting weights. He grabbed the old man by the collar and pulled him out of the seat. "How many times do I need to tell you to behave yourself?" He pushed him toward the door without acknowledging Daniel in the least—Daniel, who, after all he had prepared, still hadn't said a single word to his grandfather.

16

≈ The Thing ≈

"Here's the thing," began Seymour.

It was the following morning and the children had gathered in the library. Their plan was to puzzle through everything until it was all figured out.

"And we won't rest until we do," he declared definitively.

"Or play, either," added Dinora, daintily popping another truffle into her mouth.

They laid their few clues on the table and Rufus, Tia's twenty-year-old cat, boasting at least a pound per year, promptly nestled down on top of them. Zoë brought out big sheets of newsprint. She had titled them "what we know to be true", "what is definitely not true", "what could be true" and finally, "possible scenarios". They began brainstorming as Zoë and Greta quickly jumped from one paper to the next, writing down all their ideas.

"We know he was a scientist. That was in the article," said Dinora.

"And that his partner was Lionel Robson," said Greta as she added her contribution to the "what we know to be true" list.

"And we know he killed him," Daniel said bluntly.

"Danny," Dinora said sharply.

"We don't know that for sure," said Greta.

"And Dr. Huntington is convinced of his innocence," added Dinora.

"Then why is he in prison? They must have had evidence."

"He could have been framed," suggested Seymour. "Dr. Huntington described him as a humanitarian—dedicated to *saving* lives."

"Then what about the money? You don't see that as proof he was up to something not quite 'humanitarian'? Think about it. If that money were legitimate it would be in a bank account not a briefcase."

"It couldn't have been him," said Zoë. "He's the one who didn't want 'Mr. P' to do it."

"Daniel? What's this?" Greta was holding up a small frame with a picture inside.

"It's my contribution to our clues," he said sourly.

"Are those the pictures from your house?" asked Dinora.

"Don't call it that," said Daniel coldly.

"What?"

"'My house'. Don't ever call it that. It's not mine. I hate it and I never want to even so much as look at it again."

"Sorry, Danny," she said meekly.

Zoë raised a questioning eyebrow at Seymour, who raised his shoulders in response. This outburst wasn't at all like the mild-mannered person they knew Daniel to be.

"Do you mind?" Greta was unhooking the picture from the frame even as Daniel indicated his indifference.

The others watched as she removed the back plate and turned the picture over. "What did you say your grandfather said when you met him?"

"He said 'melons' and 'flowers'," Daniel reported, clearly embarrassed.

"'Melons' or 'melon'?" Greta clarified.

Daniel paused for a moment. "No, you're right. It was 'melon'. Why?"

She read the writing on the back of the old photograph. "Me and Melonhead, age three."

"Maybe it's not me," Daniel said.

"Danny, it *is* you," Dinora implored. "It's obviously you. And that must have been his nickname for you. That's why he remembers it, even now after all these years."

"You don't have to do this, you know. He's nothing to me. He can rot in jail for all I care."

"But look at the facts, Daniel," said Seymour. "Does he really seem like that kind of person?"

"How is that 'looking at the facts' exactly?" Daniel laughed but there was meanness in it. "You might as well give it up. My only living relative is a murderer. I've accepted that. I've moved on. Why don't you?"

After a long pause and a slowing of Daniel's breathing, Dinora asked quietly, "And what if he isn't, Danny? What if he didn't hurt anyone—didn't do what they said? What kind of friends would we be if we didn't at least try to help?" She waited a few more moments before adding softly, "What kind of grandson would you be?"

This thought brought Daniel up short, ricocheting around in him until he turned to the others, managed a resigned smile and said, in a significantly calmer fashion, "Okay, let's at least have a look."

Seymour slapped him heartily on his back as the others cheered.

"So I was wondering something else," Dinora brought them back to their task at hand. "Remember

The House was so messy? If he were a scientist, he would be a lot more organized than that. Don't get me wrong—scientists keep everything in piles all over the place. Believe me, I live with two of them. Our house is a mess but in an incredibly *organized* kind of way."

"What do you mean?" asked Greta

"Well it *looks* like a mess to everyone else but Papi and Mario know exactly where everything is. Plus, in their labs, it's—oh, Greta, what's that word when something is really, really clean? Emaciated?"

"Immaculate."

"Exactly."

"So someone else was at The House, looking for something," said Zoë. She grabbed some more paper and taped it on the large stone mantle. She took a red permanent marker and outlined a box on the far left side which she then labeled, "the thing".

"Yes," said Greta, but everyone else looked confused.

Zoë explained, "We have to think of this *linearly*—cause and effect. If someone were looking for 'something' then 'the thing' is where the timeline must start."

"So there's this 'thing' and someone wants it," confirmed Seymour.

"And maybe others know about it," added Dinora.

"And even if my grandfather didn't have it, someone thought he might," said Daniel, and the others smiled at his participation.

Zoë took this opportunity to once again broach the subject of Dr. Huntington. "Didn't anyone else think it was strange how your pal George asked Daniel if his grandfather 'left him anything'? *George* could be the one looking for 'the thing'!" She punctuated this by striking the box she'd drawn earlier. The marker went right through the paper.

"Easy, girl. Easy."

"I'm not a horse, Seymour."

"I'm sure Dr. Huntington was just trying to think of a way to help Danny," said Dinora. "He cares about him."

"Never mind," Zoë grumbled. "So we're not sure what 'the thing' is or who might be looking for it but we do know something about the order of events. To start, if Daniel's grandfather wouldn't leave his place like that, then he must have been out of the picture *before* The House was trashed."

Daniel approached the paper and picked up another marker. He drew a line coming from "the thing" and extending across the page. "Then *here* would be when my grandfather was gone and *here* The House is trashed."

"And the box must have been put there after that. The placement seemed so intentional," said Seymour.

Zoë added some more notes to their timeline, narrating as she wrote. "This also means that whatever it was Mr. P did for the money had also been done before."

"So probably it was Mr. P who put the box on the counter," said Daniel.

"Either that or someone who wanted to help your grandfather," said Seymour. "Whoever it was, they must have known The House would be ransacked and waited until afterward to bring the box. What were the ransackers hoping to find? What is 'the thing'?"

"Maybe it's the box," said Daniel.

Zoë snorted. "It's some baby stuff and other junk. I don't see how—oh, and the money."

Daniel winced.

"Someone must have thought the other stuff was valuable too. Otherwise they wouldn't have made a point of boxing it up," said Seymour.

"Maybe they put it there to disguise the key," said Daniel.

"I suppose," Seymour said thoughtfully. "But it doesn't seem random. It seems as if it should mean something—that it would mean something—to your grandfather maybe."

"We still need to confirm when this all took place," said Daniel. "Greta, you didn't remember the date from the newspaper by any chance?"

"Sorry," she answered from the stacks where she had returned to sift through books.

"Have you found anything, Greta?" Dinora asked cheerily.

"Do you *see* anything?" Zoë muttered.

"Not yet," sighed Greta. "But there's something nagging at me—something I've read—or at least seen before. I hope I recognize it when I see it."

Dinora took out a small yellow notepad and flipped to a clean page. "I'll make a to-do list," she announced, and once she had appropriately titled the page, she added "find book on Tia's shelf". As she flipped back the pages, she yelped.

"What is it?" asked Seymour.

"I took some notes from the library. I thought they might come in handy," she said proudly.

"And would you care to share?" said Zoë.

"Happy to! Well, I don't have the date of the newspaper from The House, for obvious reasons. Because I didn't remember to look and I didn't have my notepad with me," she clarified. "But I did note the day your grandfather was arrested. It was April 3rd."

Zoë added the date in parentheses after "grandfather gone".

"Here's another date." Seymour held up the ticket stub. "It's for a 7pm show on April *2nd*."

"That's when the murder happened—the newspaper said so," Dinora blurted.

"Did it say what time?"

"I don't remember. Sorry."

"Wait a second," Seymour said. "Look at this, all of you."

Greta took off her sweater and used it to save her place on the shelf. She joined the others at the table where Seymour had laid out three pieces of paper: the address on the box, the note from the bank and the mysterious letter they'd received less than two weeks before. "Notice anything?" Seymour asked.

"It's all the same handwriting," said Zoë.

"Definitely," said Daniel. "Look at the '3' and how he wrote the 'T's together."

"But this one is a little shakier, don't you think?" asked Seymour.

"Perhaps it was written when Mr. P was much older," Greta suggested.

"So Mr. P is the same person who did the thing Daniel's grandfather didn't want him to do, got the money, put half in a safety deposit box, wrote the note, put the key in the box, waited until after The House had been trashed and then left the box," Zoë stated definitively.

"He wouldn't have just left it there, though. That doesn't make any sense. If he knew my grandfather was gone and there was no family, he wouldn't just leave it."

"Maybe he planned to come back but something happened," said Dinora.

Seymour shook his head. "No, because years later he wrote the letter with the address. He must have thought the box wasn't there and then realized it had never been delivered."

"After all those years? What was he doing in the meantime?" Zoë accused, as if the man himself was in the room.

"Maybe he was in hiding. Maybe he took his half of the money and moved to Cancún. I remember an episode of *Mis Secretos* where Don Pablo cheats his partner out of all his money and then escapes with Lucia to Cancún but then Lucia's husband, who thought she was dead, finds a plane ticket and realizes the truth. Meanwhile—"

"The ticket," Daniel interrupted. "The ticket. The ticket. The movie ticket," he repeated as he picked up the sleeping Rufus to reach for the small piece of paper. "It was from the same day as the murder. What if Mr. P put it in the box to prove my grandfather was innocent?"

"If he knew he was innocent and had proof, why wouldn't he just take it to the police?" argued Seymour.

"Because he had just committed a crime—maybe robbed a bank or something, so he left it for someone else to use."

"But no one found it. Oh, Danny, that's too sad. Your grandfather in jail year after year knowing that he didn't do anything wrong and knowing his grandson, his only family, was growing up without him and not knowing how he was doing. Oh, I could simply cry."

"So cry," said Zoë.

"Zoë!" Seymour barked, following with a quick succession of something in Mandarin.

Zoë glared icily at Seymour, threw her marker at him and stormed out of the room.

"I can't cry now," Dinora assured the others, putting her shoulders back and her head up. "Some scoundrel has framed my friend's grandfather and I'm on the case!"

17

❧ The Assignment ❧

The assignments had been drawn up the previous night. This morning it was simply a matter of deciding who would do what. But before they could do this, another problem presented itself.

"She's M.I.A.!" Dinora wailed, running into the dining room for breakfast.

"Huh?" grunted Seymour.

"Zoë. She's M.I.A. That means 'missing in action'. She wasn't in her bed this morning and I can't find her anywhere!"

"Where exactly have you looked?" asked Daniel, a subtle smile playing on his lips.

Dinora thought for a moment, then tried to whisper inconspicuously, "Well I haven't exactly looked very many places but I just have a *feeling*, you know? In my gut." She said this last part as she tapped the side of her head.

"It's true." Greta entered, significantly calmer than Dinora, and ladled some steaming congee into a bowl. "Zoë's bed is made and she's nowhere to be found." She preempted Seymour's question. "I walked both the second and third floor hallways calling her name. Nothing."

"That's strange," said Daniel.

"It's not strange at all. She's just mad. She seems mad all the time now. Doesn't she? And irritable too."

"And a little suspicious," Daniel added defensively.

Dinora took a sip of hot chocolate and looked pensive. "I hadn't noticed," she said and the others turned as one, amazed by what was either her complete obliviousness or sheer optimism.

It's probably a combination, thought Greta and the others' thoughts were not dissimilar.

Edith entered the dining room and Dinora shot out of her chair.

"Edith! Zoë's gone A.W.O.L. That's when you go away without leave—like as in permission!" Even her explanation, unnecessary as it was, had been yelled.

"Maybe she needed a break," Edith responded, without slowing down.

Dinora looked confused. "From what? We're on vacation."

"Don't waste your energy, Dinora," Seymour began. "Zoë's going to sulk for as long as she wants and I for one am not going to give her the satisfaction of letting it ruin our plans. Boy, she can be such a baby."

"And what's she got against Dr. Huntington? She doesn't even know him," said Daniel.

Not even Dinora could find a positive spin on this.

"Leave it. We've got enough to worry about today— especially since there will now be only four of us."

A look from Daniel silenced any further conversation and the children rushed through their breakfast so they could gather back in the library. They had packed their clues away and rolled up the papers the night before, just in case Edith or Tia came in. There was no need to unroll them now. They each knew perfectly well what the options were. They stared out the window onto the hayfields below. No one spoke.

"I *really* don't want to do it," Daniel broke the silence. "More than that . . . I can't. I'm sorry. I can't do it. I can't go back there."

"That's okay, Danny. We know that," soothed Dinora. "Seymour, why don't the three of us go?"

"It won't work. Especially with Zoë gone, the only way to get everything done today is to split up."

No one suggested taking an extra day. Ever since they had accepted that Daniel's grandfather had been falsely imprisoned, it had been difficult to get the image of him in jail out of their minds. Each additional day, each hour even, was heartbreaking—and not just for Daniel.

"Seymour, you're the oldest," Dinora said. "It's probably best that you go."

"I was afraid someone would say that. Now I *really* wish Zoë were here. All I'd have to do is say, 'plus, I'm a boy' and she would have gone herself, just to prove she could do it." He deepened his voice and stuck out his chest. The others waited anxiously for him to accept.

He wouldn't have to say it, Greta thought about her brave friend. *She would volunteer.* Greta was reminded again about the O.G.D. and the plans she had for this summer. *No one said it was going to be easy.* "I'll go," she whispered.

The shocked expressions were almost comical and Greta smiled wanly in response. This was the part of the conversation where they were supposed to insist that she didn't have to do this, that someone else, like Seymour, would do it. No one did and Greta was both disappointed and relieved at the same time. Her only consolation was that her assignment didn't involve water.

"But Greta, The House is so *creepy*," Dinora shivered as she spoke.

"Dinora," warned Seymour.

"Sorry."

"Are you sure, Greta?" asked Seymour.

"I'm sure it's the right thing. Daniel is the only one who can ask the Ingrahams if they knew his grandfather, which means you need to be the one to go to the courthouse—you or Daniel, anyway. There's no way they're going to hand over a case file to a little girl."

"True," agreed Seymour. "They still might not give it to me, even if it is a public record."

"That's for sure," said Daniel. "Zoë and I had a miserable time trying to get information on The House and that was only a real estate record." Daniel looked right at Greta, his gratitude so clear that his words were mere reiteration. "Thank you."

"Then it's settled," said Seymour. "Let's get what we need and head down to the truck. Greta, we'll meet back up by teatime."

She nodded—afraid if she opened her mouth to speak that something else, like "please don't go" would come out.

Zoë stared at the parsonage, steeling herself for what she was about to do. She walked up the stairs and rang the doorbell. Seconds later, the door was opened by an enthusiastic preacher's wife, already dressed and raring to go, despite the fact it was barely eight o'clock.

"Well good morning! Zoë, you are a sight for sore eyes and looking lovelier than ever. Well I shouldn't say 'ever'. The other night at the dance . . . my, my, my. Weren't you just the prettiest thing? My Eli certainly thought so. And all dressed up. I couldn't believe it. I just couldn't believe it. Zoë Chen in a dress. A dress! Truth be told, child, I didn't even think you *had* legs. And to think—"

"Mother," Eli interrupted as he approached the door. "You haven't even invited her in."

"Oh, dear. Where are my manners? Come in, dear. Have a seat."

"She might like some coffeecake, Mother."

"Oh, of course. Would you like that, Zoë? And a cup of tea perhaps?"

"Uh, sure. Thank you, Mrs. Eaton."

The woman left, eager to complete her task quickly so as not to miss anything.

Eli probably knew this and graciously wasted no time. "Sorry about that."

"Don't worry. I get it all the time."

Eli considered this and quickly came to the conclusion that the remark stemmed from experience and not vanity. "So, I don't mean to be rude and I am glad to see you, but—"

"What am I doing here?"

"You don't have to tell me anything but my mother is very quick and we probably have less than a minute before she gets back. So if there's anything you'd like to say—"

"Will you go sailing with me?" Zoë blurted.

Eli's surprise was evident but he recovered quickly enough. "Sure. I'd love that. Whe—"

"Now."

"Now? Like, right now?"

"Yes." She looked at him, not trying to persuade him but her face doing the job anyway.

Eli's plans for the day went right out the window. "Okay," he said.

"Great, thank you. Let's go."

"Go where?" Mrs. Eaton was back and carrying a tea tray. "Where are you crazy kids off to?"

"Sailing, Mother. I'll see you this afternoon." Eli grabbed the large piece of coffeecake with one hand and Zoë's elbow with the other.

Together they bolted for the door. As they cleared shouting distance of the house, Eli passed the cake to Zoë. She accepted it gladly, having missed breakfast in her rush to leave Tia's that morning.

She grinned at Eli. "Nicely done."

They slowed to a brisk walk and soon found themselves aboard *The Prudence*.

"Where are we headed?" Eli asked excitedly, as they got the boat ready.

"Oh, I don't know," said Zoë casually. "Anywhere is fine."

"Why don't we head over to Isle au Haut?"

"Or Rockland. Yes, I agree. Rockland it is."

Eli looked confused but didn't have much time to ponder as Zoë was soon issuing orders.

"Uh, Zoë?"

"Yeah?"

"I've been sailing before. Many times in fact."

"Oh, sorry. I guess I'm used to hanging out with Dinora too much."

"I like that kid. She's so perky."

"Oh, she's a kick in the pants all right."

They worked in comfortable silence, saying little as they made their way across the water. Eli seemed smart enough to recognize that Zoë wasn't exactly in a chatty mood and this elevated her regard for the boy. When they had moored the boat, an hour later, he spoke. "So, now that we're in Rockland, what do you want to do? Can I buy you lunch?"

"Sure," she answered absentmindedly as they disembarked.

"Great. I know this place downtown—serves wonderful crab rolls."

"Uh huh." Zoë was already wandering toward the center of town. "Wait," she said, turning to look at him. "Where is it?"

"Downtown, on Third. Their lemonade is really good too—homemade."

"You sound like Dinora."

"Is she a big food person?"

"That's putting it mildly. So, Third? Third and what?"

"Broadway, why?"

"Broadway. Perfect," she murmured to herself. Remembering she was not alone, Zoë tried to mask her interest. "Oh, I just like to know where I'm going, that's all. In case we get separated."

Eli gave her a skeptical look.

"It could happen," she retorted.

"Uh, Zoë?" Eli stopped walking.

The distracted girl took a few more steps, realized she'd lost her companion and turned around. "What is it?"

"Look, it's not that I'm complaining—I mean, I'm having a great time." He hesitated, trying to think of a delicate way to ask his question before deciding delicacy would probably be wasted on a girl like this. "Other than needing another person to sail *The Prudence*, is there some reason you asked me to come?" he asked.

Zoë seemed to consider the thoughtlessness of her invitation for the first time. "I'm sorry, Eli," she said quietly, sincerely. "It's just that there's something I need to do and I knew none of the others would help me."

"But you thought I would," he confirmed.

She nodded. "At the dance, you . . . well, you seemed like a nice enough guy."

At this, Eli threw back his head and laughed.

Zoë couldn't help but smile. It was a great laugh and made her appreciate Eli's good nature. *He's not mad*, she thought. *He's not resentful*. She blushed, embarrassed as she accepted the harsh truth of how she would have reacted if the situation were reversed. *I'd be angry. And I'd spend the rest of the day making sure he knew it*.

"A 'nice enough guy'," Eli repeated. "Wow, Zoë. With sweet talk like that, no wonder you have boys falling at your feet."

This time she smiled more broadly. "Okay, I get it," she said, starting to laugh herself. "On second thought, I guess you're a *very* nice guy." She looked him squarely in the face, her expression softening.

"I've been upgraded," he said, again being caught off guard by just how incredibly beautiful she was. Eli stopped laughing.

Zoë leaned closer, tilted her head up and kissed him lightly on the cheek. "Thank you."

Eli Eaton was silent. It took more than a moment for his world to stop spinning. "So what's this *something* we need to do?" he asked, taking her hand in his. He gave it a subtle squeeze and released it. "And more importantly, can we eat first?"

Zoë relaxed and let her indignation from the previous night's argument recede. "Eating first is fine, especially if your restaurant is near *Haverhill Chemicals*."

"I believe it's right across the street. Why? Are we spying on them?" he said clandestinely.

She laughed, shoving him playfully. "Stop goofing off," she chided. "This is serious."

"Yes, ma'am," he saluted. "So what are they up to?"

"Well, I don't know about 'they' necessarily. But there's one man—I can't tell you his name so let's just refer to him as *Creep of the Century*—who is definitely up to no good."

"And we're hoping to catch him in the act?"

Zoë shrugged. "I know it's not the best plan. It's probably futile. For one thing, he's too slick to get caught. But, Eli, I have to try. I don't know what else to do."

"Then try we will," he declared resolutely. "Who knows? Maybe he'll be having lunch at the restaurant."

18

❧ The Quest ❦

Greta watched her friends drive away and tried to pull herself together. *Step by step,* she thought. *I just need to do this step by step. First step, stand up.* She did this. *Second step, go to the—oh, no.* She realized then she had just accidently volunteered to do something altogether more terrifying than she had first thought. Her job was to go to The House. To go and check the date on the newspaper. This would establish the timeline and they needed to know for sure. Greta was determined to be brave. Brave like Zoë. What she had forgotten was *how* she was supposed to get there.

Greta walked toward the stable. She knew theoretically how to do this. She'd watched the others do it plenty of times—although she wasn't sure if it counted if your eyes were closed in fear. She made her way to Pumpkin, a chestnut mare with a tinge of auburn in her coat and easily the most docile of Tia's horses, other than the ancient Clydesdale, which Edith called "Old Goat". Greta considered taking the old horse instead, but since she'd never actually seen him move at more than a walk, she had to accept the fact that if she wanted to get there before dark, she'd need an animal with a little more pep. She reached up to unhook the door and Pumpkin's wet lips were immediately upon her. Greta screamed and ran out of the barn.

When her nerves had settled somewhat, she looked back inside. Pumpkin's head was tilted to the side in a pose of curiosity. Greta made two more attempts before deciding that one incredibly brave thing was just going to have to be enough for today. She grabbed her backpack and started out across the fields.

After the first hour, she wished she had tried a fourth time to ride Pumpkin. After the second hour, all she could think of was how wonderful it would feel to be atop a horse and cantering across the meadow. After the third hour, her sore feet, her headache from the broiling sun and her longing for a drink from a long-empty water bottle, finally got the best of her. Greta sat down with a frustrated thump and began to sob. The crying helped and after about five minutes of it, with no one the wiser, Greta looked around, rose and made her way down the hill. She entered the woods at nearly the same spot as they had the time before. Then, it had been a great adventure—exciting and beautiful. Now the forest seemed gloomy and eerily quiet. The trees had changed shape and she began to second guess herself. *Maybe this wasn't the same place. Maybe I've entered at the wrong point. I could be lost. I am lost. I'm lost.*

Then she heard the most marvelous sound. It was a gurgle. A glorious and welcome sound indeed! She followed it and in moments she had reached the large stream. This was the exact spot, for there was the make-shift bridge, the large granite boulder. Everything as it had been before. Her spirits buoyed, she flitted across, approached the water, filled her bottle, washed her face and arms, took long gulps of the icy delicious drink and felt all of these things soar through her, rejuvenating her body and spirit. She took off her sandals and gingerly dipped her feet in. It was freezing, and although she could only stand it for seconds at a time, it felt like heaven. She closed her eyes and rested a moment, allowing herself this brief respite before completing the most arduous part of her journey.

It's not that difficult, she reasoned. *I've just hiked three hours—all the way across the island. This is a short walk. I get to The House, I go in, I grab the paper, I leave. Done. Ten minutes. Even less if I hurry. Ten minutes and I'm back here, by this lovely stream. Ten minutes and I'm brave.*

It was this last thought that did it. She used the hem of her summer frock to dry her feet before replacing her sandals. She stood up and began walking determinedly toward The House. She found it more quickly than she had expected. Greta gazed at the sheer botanical wall from across the field and played with her perspective until she was able to distinguish the subtle contours of the cottage within. It didn't look nearly as scary as she had remembered, or more precisely, as she had re-envisioned. This was the price of an active imagination.

She knew it wasn't "now or never" but that's what she told herself. "Ready . . . set . . . *go!*" she whispered and on the last word she shot across the open field, darting between the strange plantings, up the driveway. In seconds she had wriggled through the wisteria into a pitch-black room. Her heart was beating with such speed that the blood roared in her ears. Greta felt as if an alarm were about to go off—as though if she didn't finish, The House would start locking itself up and she'd be trapped. *A torch! Oh, no!* She had forgotten how dark it would be. There was no time for this. No time for reprimands. She had to think. *Think!* She went to the window through which she had entered the last time and where the others had pulled away the foliage. She tore open the curtains. They collapsed in a heap of dust. She started choking, reached for her canteen and took a gulp of stream water.

She opened her eyes. The dust had settled and the early afternoon sun, which had scalded her less than an hour before, was now burning through the window with the same blessed intensity. It shone directly on the table. The newspaper was there. She grabbed it and turned toward the window. And as she did, her eyes locked on his.

It was a man.

It was *the* man—the one from the café in Bangor. The one Zoë said was following them. He was just outside The House, staring at it. Staring . . . at her.

There was no use hiding. By the expression on his face, it was clear he had seen her. Her mind began racing. *There's another way out—the kitchen!* She ran for it, slamming her shin into the corner of a coffee table. She cried out in pain. She moved more slowly, feeling her way through the dark room as quickly as she could. What was that noise? Was it the man? He was shouting. Calling. Something. Was he closer or farther away? She couldn't tell. *Don't faint, don't faint, don't—*

"No!" she screamed with a fierceness born out of both desperation and determination. She ran through the kitchen, not caring what she hit. She tore through the side door and out into the open air. She didn't stop to see where he was. She bolted into the woods.

"Hey!" he called, starting to run after her.

He's faster but I'm smaller. He's faster but I'm smaller. Greta moved furtively behind trees, making no sound. He entered the woods and began raising a ruckus. Branches cracking underfoot, heavy breathing, leaves rustling. She used these sounds as her reverse beacon— gradually working her way farther from them. Then realization hit. *I'm on the wrong side of The House.* She readjusted her course, keeping The House within just enough eyesight so as not to lose her point of reference. Her pursuer continued to bungle around.

"Aah!" Greta screamed as an unnoticed, but nevertheless extremely sharp, tree branch grazed her cheek and stabbed her neck. She pulled away and immediately felt the skin tear. Warm blood began to trickle out of the wound.

The man spun around and made his way toward her. Fortunately enough for the moment, the straightest path was blocked by bushes and fallen trees. The man was wearing a suit and it was taking him awhile to get past all of it. There was no point in hiding now. Greta darted out of the woods and across the field. The man was yelling incoherently after her. Now she was back among the trees but this time on the correct side. She careened through the forest until she reached the stream. She hopped the three stone steps, keeping pressure on her neck with one hand and holding her backpack with the other. In her haste she didn't see the wet leaves on the third rock. The moment her foot touched them and twisted, she knew things were about to get much worse. Down she went into the freezing water but not quite all of her. Her upper torso and her right elbow landed on the second rock.

"No!" she cried. "Not again, not again," she repeated as she worked through the pain. She struggled against the current, from rock to rock—half swimming and half pushing. She made it to the other side and crawled out.

"Little girl!" It was the man. He was running toward the bridge. "Come back here! Come back here this instant!"

Greta drew on some inner strength. She ran to her end of the bridge and began to push the birches off the bank. They fell quickly and were instantly carried downstream. When she had disabled the bridge, she looked up to see that the man had just reached the granite boulder bisecting the stream. He looked around, realizing he was unable to go any farther—at least not on this path. He reached into his breast pocket and began pulling something out.

Greta didn't wait to see what it was. She turned and ran faster than she ever had before. Legs pumping, blood pumping, the wound in her neck pumping but she didn't care. Soon she was out of the woods and climbing the hill. She didn't risk a look back, terrified to be hurt again.

Now everything took its toll. The heat, the exhaustion, the fear. The bruises, the fall, the memories. The rush of adrenaline, the utter depletion of it. The gash in her neck and the blood covering her hand, seeping through her clothes. She barely made her way to the top of the hill, knowing it would be impossible to go any farther. She collapsed.

"Greta!" someone screamed. She turned. It wasn't the man. It couldn't be. He didn't know her name. Who was it?

It was a girl.

Zoë and Sophocles thundered toward her, clumps of dust and grass flying behind them. When they reached her, Zoë sharply reined in the horse and he reared, just like in the movies. As soon as all four hooves were on the ground, the girl jumped off. "What happened?" she demanded.

"We need to get away," Greta wheezed. "There's someone after me."

Zoë's actions were virtually instantaneous. For the second time that summer and the second summer in a row, she picked up Greta's frail body and swung it over her shoulder. She transferred her to the horse, which stopped prancing and held still, sensing the urgency. "Hyah!" she shouted the moment her feet were in the stirrups. She wrapped one arm around Greta's torso as the girl clung to the saddle. Zoë used her other hand to yank the reins to the right, turning the horse around. She heeled Sophocles hard. "Hyah, hyah."

The horse didn't waste any time. He galloped mightily across the island, carrying the girls to safety.

Greta turned to face her hero. "Zoë, I didn't faint."

The older girl smiled broadly. "No, Greta. You didn't faint."

"I'm brave," she said before succumbing to exhaustion.

19

❧ The Office ❧

It had started raining the night before—a solid summer rain, simultaneously warm and torrential. It lasted through the night and by morning showed no signs of stopping.

"Well, no market today," said Daniel.

This, at least, was good news. Although it wasn't a chore they minded, it was a chore nonetheless and a day free—even a rainy day—would be appreciated. After breakfast they met back at headquarters, which is how they'd come to think of Tia's library. Greta, fully restored from the previous day's adventures and brimming with pride over her accomplishment, had resumed her role as book-searcher.

Daniel was carefully unfolding the aged newspaper, which had gotten soaked in her fall. "Don't worry," he assured her. "Your efforts were not in vain, Greta. I'll find the date. It'll just take a little time."

"You can't rush these things," Dinora added. "At least, that's what I've heard."

"Zoë, would you care to share what productive thing *you* did yesterday for our noble cause?" asked Seymour, in a snide tone.

"Well, let me see," his cousin began, just as spiteful. "I suppose the most *productive* thing I did yesterday was picking wildflowers in the meadow." Her voice turned sweet. "Other than that, it would have been rescuing my friend from the danger you all put her in." Zoë's words ended hard. Yesterday, when she had returned to find the others sipping tea and waiting for Greta—whom they had assured her "should be back any minute"—Zoë was irritated.

Her irritation quickly changed to fury, however, when she'd discovered where they'd sent the youngest of the children. "How could you?" she berated. "You sent her to a ramshackle haunted house? On foot?"

It was only then that the others had considered Greta might not have taken a horse.

"Aargh!" Zoë had clutched the sides of her head, as if trying to prevent it from exploding in anger and incredulity. "Oh for Pete's sake," she'd groused, stomping out of the room and heading for the stables.

Even now, a day and an explanation later, she fumed. "Don't start with me, Seymour." She didn't deign to look at him. "I'm not in the mood."

Seymour harrumphed in a truly Zoë-like fashion and turned back to his project. After nearly an entire day working through the red tape of small-town bureaucracies, he had been able to retrieve a file on the case. Unfortunately, it was too sparse to be of much use.

Dinora was hard at work on her movie stub. At the library she had sifted through mammoth phone books from the surrounding areas, looking up theaters in each of them. Once she'd weeded out the ones not ending in the "co" from the ticket stub, she had eleven. With some additional research and a significant amount of help from the new librarian, Miss Emma Darling, she was able to rule out the ones built in the last ten years. Arranging the remaining establishments in the order of distance, she chose three as the most likely. "There's *Phillip's Films co.* in Bangor, *Teatro Flamenco* in Rockland and—this one's my favorite—*Cinema Magnifico*!" she said with a dramatic flourish. "That one's in Belfast. I think we should check out Rockland first. It's the closest."

"And what? Walk up with an old ticket stub and see if they'll let us in?" asked Zoë.

"Well, no," said Dinora. "But we could show it to the owner and maybe he could tell us more."

"That's a stupid idea."

"Zoë!" snapped Seymour.

"What?"

He looked at her imploringly but her expression was implacable. "Never mind," he sighed.

Greta wasn't particularly making great headway on her search and recognized another opportunity to help their efforts. "Zoë, will you teach me Mandarin?"

The others stopped what they were doing to look at Greta, then Zoë.

"Uh, Greta, I'm not sure that's such a good idea," cautioned Dinora.

"Yeah," Seymour agreed. "I'm happy to teach you some words, Greta."

"She didn't ask *you* though, did she?" Zoë bit back as she continued to look appraisingly at her petitioner. "It depends," she said slowly, almost suspiciously. "Why do you want to learn?"

Greta considered this for a moment before stating confidently. "I want to be able to speak as well as you."

Zoë seemed to consider this. "Are you sure?" she asked.

Greta didn't respond. Some people were bothered by this idiosyncrasy of hers, in which she tended not to reiterate information that had already been established.

Zoë found her brevity refreshing.

"In Mandarin there are four tones," she began, with no other introduction. She nodded toward a small table at the other end of the room and Greta followed her there. Zoë grabbed some paper and pens. "This is important. If you get them wrong you could end up calling your mother a horse."

Greta proved herself to be a remarkable student to Zoë's great and obvious satisfaction. The girls spent the rest of the morning going over grammatical structure. Greta wasn't bored once. She had always loved words and now there were even more of them.

With Zoë thus distracted the others were able to accomplish a fair amount of work, or at least as much as the little information they'd added would allow. When they went down to make some lunch, they honored Daniel's wishes and didn't discuss their work.

"Dinora, why didn't you ever try to learn Mandarin?" Greta asked, as she stuffed some sprouts and falafel into her pita bread.

"Oh, two languages are enough for me. Already it gets so confusing. Sometimes I think in Spanish and speak in English. Then I mix them up and it turns to Spanglish. I don't know what would happen if I tried to fit one more in." She laughed, "Maybe it'd be Spanglisharin."

"And I thank my lucky stars for that every day," said Zoë. "It's the only language where I can get a little peace and quiet."

"That's mean," reprimanded Seymour.

"What? She knows I'm kidding."

Seymour sighed audibly.

"Zoë, the weather's clearing. We're thinking about sailing this afternoon," said Daniel. "Do you want to come?"

The girl looked skeptically at the two boys. "Sure," she said hesitantly.

The children polished off their lunches, cleaned up their mess and gathered the few things they'd need. In less than an hour they were on *The Prudence*, Zoë at the helm.

"Where to?" Zoë asked, as Daniel approached her.

"Rockland," he responded casually.

Zoë didn't say anything but Daniel noticed her knuckles whitening on the wheel.

It was a tense trip and even the ocean didn't seem to relax them. As they approached the moorage, Seymour took charge.

"So we need more information. The case file we got was pretty pitiful but the trial did take place in Rockland." He avoided looking at Zoë. "I figure half of us try the Rockland Courthouse and see if we can get more information on the case."

"And the others can go to *Teatro Flamenco* and see if anyone remembers a person who saw a movie there ten years ago," added Dinora, without any trace of cynicism.

Zoë feigned indifference. "So who's going with whom?"

"That depends," Seymour responded tightly. "Which one do you want to do?"

Zoë looked at Dinora's eager face. "I'll go to the courthouse."

"I'll come with you," offered Greta.

"Great," said Zoë, not taking her narrowing eyes off Seymour. "You're up to something," she accused.

"Yes, Zoë, I am. I'm up to trying to solve this mystery and get Daniel's grandfather out of jail. Anytime you feel like helping we wouldn't mind in the least."

Zoë gave her cousin a cursory glare, then headed off. "*Zou ba*, Greta."

The two girls made their way down the wharf, toward the center of town.

Greta didn't waste any time. "Zoë, why don't you like Dinora?"

"Huh?"

Greta was silent. She knew Zoë had heard her.

"What makes you say that?"

Again, no response.

"I like her plenty. She's like a sister to me, you know. Annoying, but you just put up with it."

"You're mean to her," said Greta quietly. She reached for Zoë's hand and guided her to the lawn of the First Congregational Church of Rockland. "You know that."

Now it was Zoë who was silent, although it was clear her mind was wrestling with something. When she did begin talking, her voice was barely above a whisper. "She's just so happy, you know? Like *all-the-time* happy. No one's that happy. It's ridiculous. It's fake. It's—oh, I don't know. I guess we're just too different, that's all."

She pulled some pieces of grass from the lawn and began plaiting them together over another stretch of silence. "Did you know that Seymour and I grew up together—like in the same house and everything?"

Greta nodded.

"Until we were five anyway. We lived in Kweilin then. Both our dads traveled a lot. Our mothers—they're sisters—thought it'd be easier to just live together—help each other out, keep each other company, you know?" There was a catch in her voice and it looked as if Zoë were about to cry. "We'd come here for the summers, just like our mothers did when they were little. It was so much fun. Not like now. Fun like being free, not having to worry." She threw the grass into the street.

"It's so stupid. I still can't believe it, can't believe they did that to us. We were everything to each other. He was more than my cousin, more than my brother even. We were the same age. In a way it was like being twins. Every day we were discovering something new but because there was someone else with you it was like finding out twice as much, learning twice as much, seeing things in two different ways but at the same time. Every day was like that. I don't know how to explain it."

"It sounds exhilarating," said Greta quietly, wrapping her arms around her legs and resting her head on her knees.

"It had been like that for as long as I could remember. Learning from each other, teaching each other. We were one person but so much more than that. We finished each other's sentences, had our own private language." Zoë's voice trailed off and she wiped her eyes with her hands. "Then it just ended." She looked at Greta. "Just like that. They didn't tell us, didn't warn us. Aargh!" she groaned and Greta got a picture of a child's frustration left to fester for ten years.

"What happened?" Greta encouraged.

"I don't know exactly. Neither of our mothers will talk about it. It probably wasn't just one thing. They're very unlike one another. I think they just couldn't get along. They never say anything about each other but you can tell they don't exactly approve of each other's choices. Their parenting styles are *very* different."

"So just like that you and Seymour were separated?"

"Yup. Seymour moved to Seattle and we stayed in China."

"That must have been so difficult for you—for both of you."

"I don't remember it now, but my father said I had nightmares for months afterward. I couldn't sleep, I didn't eat, I wouldn't play with other kids. It felt like someone had stolen half of me."

Greta clasped the older girl's hand in hers.

Zoë stood up, brushed off her jeans, wiped her eyes again and turned to help Greta up. "We've got work to do. Let's get to the courthouse."

They made their way toward the tall imposing building at the end of State Street. As they crossed Seventh Avenue, Zoë stopped in the middle of the road and muttered to herself. "That sneaky little—I *knew* he was up to something!"

"What?"

"C'mon," ordered Zoë, spinning her around and running down the street.

The Office

It was all Greta could do to keep up. "Zoë, what's happening?"

The girl stopped and waited for Greta to catch her breath. "Remember the article in the library? It said the trial was at the new courthouse. The *new* courthouse. This one has been around forever." She motioned vaguely to the building they had just left. "The *new* courthouse is in Belfast."

"So Seymour was mistaken?"

"Hah! He wasn't mistaken about anything. He was trying to ditch us. Well good luck with that, cuz." Zoë headed off again with the determination of someone who knew exactly where she was headed and why.

Within minutes they reached their destination and Greta stared at the large building with exquisite landscaping. The golden letters emblazoned across the main doors read: *Haverhill Chemicals*. Zoë marched in. The marble foyer housed a young woman with hair done up in the latest fashion and she looked as if it was her hairstyle that demanded most of her thinking.

"May I help you?" the popinjay of a receptionist asked.

"You may," declared Zoë. "Which office here belongs to George Huntington?"

"And do you have an appointment?"

"You bet I do."

This seemed to fluster the young woman. "Well, Dr. Huntington is in Suite 400, on the top floor but—"

"Thanks," Zoë called. An elevator had deposited a rider and the two girls managed to slip in just as the doors were closing.

When they re-opened, Greta noticed the top floor was even fancier than the lobby. It made her self-conscious about their faded jeans and salty smell. Zoë didn't seem the least distracted. She marched to the door marked *400* and banged loudly.

"Come in," said a smooth voice, not at all alarmed by the rude disruption.

Zoë swung open the door and there they were—Daniel, Seymour and Dinora, taking tea in the roomy luxurious office of her nemesis. "Well, well, well," she said. "So *this* is how it is?"

"Miss Chen," Dr. Huntington rose and motioned for her and Greta to take a seat. "Miss Washington. It's so nice of you to join us."

"Hmph," grunted Zoë, showing no intention of moving a muscle.

"Dr. Huntington was just offering to help us get the full case file," said Daniel excitedly.

"Well I can't promise anything," he gave Daniel a warm smile. "But I can at least try. And, I also promised," he stood up elegantly, "to show you the view from the executive balcony. Miss Washington, would you care to join us?" Dr. Huntington maneuvered himself so as to block Zoë.

She yawned exaggeratedly. "If you've seen one view, you've seen them all. I'll meet you guys downstairs."

"Oh, but you'll still come, Greta," urged Dinora. "It'll be spectacular."

Dr. Huntington corralled the children into the hallway. "And then afterward I'll treat you all to lunch across the street. Their food is wonderful. In fact, I believe some of you may have eaten there recently." He didn't look at Zoë but his meaning was clear.

Seymour, picking up on it right away, hung back and stared accusingly at his cousin. "What, so now you've stooped to spying on someone who's trying to help us?" he said under his breath. She pressed the "down" button and just stared at the elevator doors. "Great, Zo. That's just great. Keep on 'helping' like this and we'll never free Daniel's grandfather." Seymour made his way toward the others, who were entering a private room at the end of the hall.

Zoë bit her lip hard to prevent herself from crying. Channeling her hurt and anger, she quickly crept back into the office and got to work. There was a big filing cabinet but she sensed anything current or confidential would be in his desk. She was right. At the very bottom of the third drawer she found the last thing she expected and the one thing that might truly make a difference.

Without a second thought, Zoë swiped it.

20

✎ The File ✎

For the next two days the children found ways to occupy themselves as they waited for Dr. Huntington to come through on his promise of help. All of their other investigations had reached impasses. The same day Greta had gone to The House, Seymour had retrieved a little information on the charges, the trial and the verdict. Daniel had spent the day talking with Dr. Ingraham and other people from The Island, trying to find out if they knew anything more about his grandfather. Out of respect for his family, most folks pretended not to remember. He hoped word wouldn't get back to Tia, but even he knew that on The Island it was more an issue of "when" than "if".

Dinora had visited the *Teatro Flamenco* when they were in Rockland the previous day. She'd shown the stub to the owner, who had looked at her as if she were crazy. Unfettered by this, Dinora simply thanked him for his time and crossed the *Teatro Flamenco* off her list, leaving only two. She considered calling the other theaters, but decided it was the kind of job better done in person. "When I can see the whites of their eyes," she said. This also made sense since there was a lack of privacy on The Island phone line and Daniel didn't want anyone to know he was trying to free his grandfather.

The only thing to do now was to wait.

The children passed the time by working in the garden, swimming in the Lily Pond and riding the horses. But none of them traveled too far from Tia's and when they were there, they spent much of their time fretting and pacing floors. This was mostly true of Daniel. Now that he was opening his heart and mind to the idea of having family again, he was a bundle of nerves.

Greta, whose temperament ran pretty level, had chosen to continue her work perusing the stacks. She scanned, book after book, trying to remember what it was that nagged at her.

Zoë was even more independent. She'd work with the others in the garden or help Edith if asked but other than that, it was self-imposed solitary confinement for her. If the other children were in the library, she'd be in the music room. If they were swimming, she'd be off with Sophocles. Much of the time she had her nose in a book and seemed determined to punish them for whatever affront they'd made. In truth, it was because of Seymour and they all knew it. Even Dinora noticed the rift growing between the cousins.

But Seymour showed no sign of backing down. "Zoë's temper," he told the others, "has gone too far. No matter what she's upset about, there's no excuse for being rude or mean—especially to people who are trying to help us. No. If any apologizing is going to be done it's going to be by her and not me. I've had enough." Seymour dove into the water. When he emerged, Greta noticed his brow was furrowed and his eyes red.

He's hurting, she thought, remembering her conversation with Zoë. She knew that Zoë was miserable too, but if there were ever two more stubborn people, Greta had never met them.

Saturday morning dawned and the children made their way into town for the farmers market.

"And look who's here," announced Zoë as she spotted Dr. Huntington getting out of his baby blue Mercedes convertible.

"Don't start, Zoë. Do you hear me?" Seymour warned.

"I'm not deaf, Seymour."

"Zoë, please?" Daniel asked. "For me. Will you just let it rest?"

Zoë looked hurt at this. "Daniel, the guy's not . . . he's not—"

"Not what?" Dr. Huntington's teeth were as white as ever. His cerulean eyes sparkled merrily and sunshine seemed to follow him wherever he went. "Not late for strawberries? I hope not." He picked one out of a box and tasted it. "Delicious," he pronounced. "That Dorothea really knows her way around a garden."

"You know Tia?" Dinora asked excitedly.

"Sure. We went to high school together—the lot of us. It's a small island. In fact, her mother was my teacher. That Mrs. Witherspoon, she didn't take guff from anyone," he laughed with the others (save Zoë who was stewing in a corner). "Good times, good times."

"Dr. Huntington, were you able to—" began Daniel.

"Danny, my boy," he said, handing over a thick manila envelope. "That's for you."

"Thank you!" Relief seemed to wash right over him.

"And that's not all."

"It's not?"

"No. I spoke with a friend of mine, man by the name of Dickson. Burl Dickson. He's a litigator. In fact, he's the best money can buy."

"And?" Daniel was bracing himself for more good news, afraid to hope but hoping with all his heart nonetheless.

"And he said he'll take your case," Dr. Huntington announced proudly. "I took the liberty of making an appointment for you—first thing Monday morning. His office is in Belfast. I put the address in the envelope."

"But I don't have any money. Barely any. I couldn't afford him."

"Danny, you've got—" began Dinora.

"Think nothing of it, Danny. I've taken care of it. Believe me, I'm just as determined as you to free your grandfather. He's a good man and we need him back here. You haven't had a chance to see him yet, have you?"

"Yes," said Daniel, reluctantly.

This got Dr. Huntington's immediate attention. "You have? How was he? What did he say?"

Daniel's cheeks flushed. "He was fine, I guess," he answered hesitantly.

"Well I suppose that's only to be expected. Still, he'll be with us soon enough and, speaking of which . . ." He put a fatherly arm around Daniel. "Do you mind if we go for a little walk?"

"I guess not." Daniel turned to the others.

"We've got it, Daniel," said Seymour. "Take as long as you need."

"Thanks."

"Daniel?" called Zoë, a look of genuine concern on her face.

He didn't bother to answer.

"You can't blame him, Zo," consoled Seymour.

"Don't tell me what I can or can't do," she spat.

Daniel and Dr. Huntington were gone for what remained of the morning. When they returned, Daniel walked Dr. Huntington to his car, where they shook hands. The older man got into his vehicle, started it and drove off—waving to Daniel.

"What happened?" Dinora asked.

"He asked me if I wanted to come live with him. Me and my grandfather, after he gets out."

The others thought about this.

"It's not like I have many options," continued Daniel. "Even if I wanted to live there, The House is ruined. And I can hardly keep my grandfather in my room at Tia's."

No one said anything.

"Well, he said it was an open offer anyway."

"Wow," said Dinora, who could think of nothing else to say.

"Hey, you can worry about that later," said Seymour, as he picked up the thick envelope. "We've got information *and* a lawyer. Let's get to work!"

Once at Tia's the children rushed upstairs. Within minutes they had taken out all of their evidence and notes. Daniel opened up the envelope and took out a file. He sat down and began going through it page by page. As he finished one, he'd pass it to Seymour, who in turn would pass it to Dinora, who in turn would murmur "hmm" and "interesting" and "you don't say" as she scribbled in her notebook.

Greta had resumed her post at the books. She had every intention of reading that file cover to cover but she wanted to wait until the others had fully mulled it over. Then she would have it all to herself and could peruse it at her own pace. Zoë, making a rare appearance, was curled up in a chair by the large window. She was reading, but clearly keeping an ear on their conversation at the same time.

"Daniel, look at this," said Seymour, passing him a piece of white paper.

"It's the police report," said Daniel.

"Exactly. Now look at this. It's the same report but from the file Dr. Huntington gave you. Look here and here."

"What is it?" asked Dinora, straining to see.

"It's the same report but the one we got has all of the confidential information blacked out." He held up the other piece of paper for the rest to see. It didn't have a black mark on it. "How could he have gotten this?"

"*Thank you!*" Zoë jumped out of the chair and charged over to Daniel. "Now do you believe me?"

"What do you mean?" He looked confused.

"He's up to something. He's not legit. He's a creep."

"Zoë, he's helping us. He's helping me," implored Daniel. "Look, this has everything, even first-hand accounts."

"But how?" She turned to her cousin. "Seymour, you yourself just said it. *How* could he have gotten all this information?"

"It almost looks like the file the prosecutor might have had," said Seymour.

"And how could he have gotten that, I wonder?" screeched Zoë.

"Dr. Huntington knows lawyers, I don't know. Zo, what's the big deal? You want us *not* to have this? This could free Daniel's grandfather!"

"You don't get it. That snake is up to something. You don't agree it's just a little strange that he always happens to run into us on *Saturdays?*"

"There have only been two."

"If he was able to get us *this*," she motioned to the thick file on the table, "it seems like he'd be powerful enough to get it to us yesterday but then he'd have to come to the house. Probably he's afraid. Doesn't want Tia or Edith to see him because they know he's a—"

"Then why would he be helping me?" argued Daniel.

"I don't know why. I'm just saying it's strange. Daniel, why can't you see that?"

"Because all I can see is my grandfather, who doesn't even know what year it is, sitting in some jail cell! Why can't *you* see *that?*" he yelled.

"Daniel, I didn't mean—"

"I don't care! I'm sick of you trying to ruin the only chance I have. If you're just going to attack the closest person I have to some real family then don't help me." He stopped yelling. "I don't need it."

"But Daniel—"

He just stared at her.

She looked around at the others, tears welling in her eyes. "Fine," she said, going back to her chair, grabbing her book and slinking out of the room.

Getting out of church the next morning was not an option for all of them, but Daniel was able to swing it. He told Tia he wasn't feeling well, which of course was true and it wasn't at all difficult for her to believe. She may have had her own worries and affairs but she was keenly attuned to the emotional well-being of her charges and it was obvious something was deeply troubling the boy.

After the other children left with Tia, Daniel, an incredibly fast runner, lit out for the ferry. He was able to walk onto the 10:05. This time he had his own money, which he'd withdrawn from his account along with enough to replace what he'd taken from the briefcase. Once the ferry had deposited him on the mainland, he jogged the remaining miles. For the second time this summer, he boarded the bus, flagged a taxi and found himself, once again, sitting across the table from his grandfather. He didn't waste any time.

"Grandfather," he whispered.

The old man didn't look up.

"Grandfather, I'm here. It's Daniel." He lowered his voice. "It's Melonhead."

This seemed to stir something. "Melonhead?" the man murmured, looking up into Daniel's eyes. "No, not my Melon, not *my* boy."

"I'm older now, Grandfather. It's been a long time. Ten years. I'm fifteen now."

"Ten years?" he reached out and let the tips of his fingers graze the boy's cheek.

Daniel smiled. "Yes."

The old man grasped his hands with an intensity Daniel wouldn't have expected in such a frail person.

"The flowers, Melon. The flowers."

"What do you mean?" Daniel asked anxiously. "I don't understand. What about the flowers?"

"The flowers, the flowers, the flowers." He released his grip and returned to his murmuring state of oblivion.

"Grandfather, I need to ask you some questions. I need to tell you some things."

The man continued to murmur, "Flowers, flowers, flowers."

"Grandfather, I've been to The House. To your house." He took a deep breath. "*Our* house. There was a box there with stuff in it." He listed off the things but nothing seemed to resonate.

"Flowers!" the man wailed, standing up and grabbing Daniel, shaking him and screaming.

Instantly, the coldhearted prison guard was there, pulling the hysterical man off Daniel and shoving him back through the door. Back to his cell.

21

❧ The Diary ❧

Tia and Edith left as soon as Sunday dinner was finished.

"We may be gone two nights, my darlings, but no more than that. No more than that. Take care of yourselves and don't get into any trouble."

"Not a stitch, Tia," promised Dinora. "Where are you going?"

"I have an errand to run, darling. Just a little errand." And with that Tia bustled toward two suitcases that had been set near the door. They must have been ready before church but the children hadn't noticed, except for Greta, who had also observed two plane tickets.

Seymour waved goodbye to the two women as they rode off in the Sunday car. "Well, we have the place to ourselves," he said, picking up a dessert plate and dipping it into the steaming soapy water. "At least we can speak freely."

Daniel rinsed and dried the dish. "I think we should visit the lawyer tomorrow morning. I've been looking through the file and all they had was circumstantial evidence. Someone heard them arguing and then the brake lines were cut on Lionel Robson's car. It drove right off the cliff on the north end of The Island. They never even found his body."

"Your grandfather must have had a really bad lawyer," said Dinora. "Danny, did he say anything this morning about it?"

"For a second there I thought he recognized me, but then he started ranting about the flowers again and they took him away."

"I'm so sorry, Danny."

"All I can hope is that once we get him out he can start getting better, but I'm not sure if people do get better from stuff like that."

"Do you think the jail made him crazy?" cringed Dinora.

"He doesn't seem crazy. Just confused and out-of-it. You think that could go away?"

No one met his eyes. Eventually Dinora said, "It could. You never know, Danny. It could."

"So we'll head over to Belfast in the morning and speak to this Burl Dickson?" Seymour confirmed.

All agreed except for Zoë, who was reading, curled up in Tia's armchair, with Rufus sprawled across her chest.

"Zoë, will you come?" Dinora asked.

"Huh?" Zoë's concentration was broken.

"What are you reading?" Seymour asked. "You've had your nose in that book ever since we got back from Rockland. What gives?"

"I'm not sure if I should tell you, Seymour. Your high moral fiber might be offended by *how* I got it."

"You stole it?" he asked incredulously.

"And what if I did?"

"What is it, Zoë?" Daniel asked, sounding much more like himself than he had the day before. "Is it important?"

She passed it to him and he began flipping through pages. "What is this? Where did you get it? Is this what I think it is, Zoë?"

The girl nodded and slowly began to smile. "It's exactly what you think it is. And it says a lot. I think this could actually help." She cast her eyes to the floor and lowered her voice. "Daniel, I hope you know . . . I hope you . . . well, I just wanted to help. That's all. I wasn't trying to make things more difficult. Really, I wasn't." Her eyes began to fill with tears. Zoë covered her face in frustration and embarrassment.

Daniel set the book on the table. He leaned closer to his friend and whispered, "It's okay, Zoë."

She looked up anxiously. "You sure?"

"Sure I'm sure." He smiled, opening his arms.

She gave a quick hug then got right back to business. "Here, let me show you this one section I found."

"Will somebody please tell me what's going on?" asked Dinora.

"Sorry, Dinora," said Zoë, moving closer and putting her arm affectionately around the girl. "For everything."

"Like what?"

Zoë could only laugh at this. "For everything, Dinora. I've just had some stuff on my mind lately. You know?"

"About the book you mean?" Dinora still looked confused.

"Never mind." Zoë wiped her remaining tears away, reached for the book and showed it to the younger girl. "It's a diary," she explained. "In fact it's the diary of Daniel's grandfather."

"Oh my!" said Dinora, understanding visibly blooming on her face. "Oh my!" she repeated.

Daniel started to read the book. "Listen to this," he said. "The last entry is dated second April 1959." He paused as recognition dawned. "That's the date of the murder."

Bruiser came by again today. That fool just can't take "no" for an answer. He can't see past the money. I tried explaining it to him but it's no use. In a way I feel sorry for Peri. He wants the money desperately. Thinks it'll bring him happiness. He doesn't even seem to care about his career, his reputation, the benefit to humanity. Unfortunately he will have to settle for the gratitude of millions instead of a million.

It'll be nice to head over to Belfast tonight and see the movie, Anatomy of a Murder. It sounds a little gruesome to me but he's eager to see it. And I always do enjoy that Jimmy Stewart.

"Why didn't you tell us you had this?" Seymour accused.

Zoë's expression looked hurt and she lashed back. "Oh, I'm sorry. I thought that's how we were doing things these days—keeping secrets from one another," she said sarcastically.

"And you stole it? From whom?"

"From your precious George!"

"Dr. Huntington?" Daniel asked.

"I can't believe you'd do that!" shout Seymour.

"Well, what was he doing with it anyway? You don't think that's strange?"

"What? Strange that a man would keep the diary of his best friend who's been imprisoned? No, I don't."

"Forget about that!" Daniel yelled at the two of them before lowering his voice. "I don't care why he had it or that you took it. This is incredible. It could tell us so much. Can we just think about that, huh?"

"Fine," Seymour snarled. "What else does it say?"

"I thought you wouldn't be interested in 'ill-gotten gains', Seymour?"

Dinora piped in before Seymour had a chance to respond. "That means the cinema was the *Cinema Magnifico*! According to my records," she tapped her notebook, "that's in Belfast. We could do both tomorrow—see the lawyer and visit the theater."

"I just don't want to tell the lawyer about the diary, okay? Dr. Huntington has been so nice to us," Daniel said, making a special point of looking intently at Zoë. "I don't want him to know we betrayed his trust."

"Hmph," grunted Zoë.

"He's talking about the thing Mr. P did," Greta said, bringing them back to the matter at hand. "Maybe Mr. P is 'Peri'. Look," she pointed to the page. "See where he says that Peri will have to 'settle for the gratitude of millions instead of *a* million'? Then Mr. P later wrote to him and said, 'I know you didn't want me to do it but here's your *half*' and he leaves him *half* a million."

"Are we certain it's half though?" asked Seymour. "I know it's around that but we haven't counted it."

"I have," Daniel said. "It's half." The tone in his voice revealed that his disgust for the money hadn't changed for the better and had quite possibly gotten worse.

"Now we're getting somewhere," said Zoë.

"What else does it say, Daniel?" asked Seymour.

"Wait," said Greta. "We should start from the beginning. That's what Mario would say. We hear it aloud from the very beginning with five sets of ears."

"He would say that," agreed Dinora.

They left the remaining dishes and gathered in the front parlor. With the whole house to themselves it didn't matter where they met and the parlor was especially sunny and filled with furniture from Tia's grandparents. It was like stepping into another world, as the room probably hadn't changed much since the house had been built more than a hundred years earlier.

Once they were settled, Daniel began reading. "*Twentieth December 1957. Felicia arrived today with a rambunctious Melonhead in tow. She's looking worn-out and I wonder*—" Daniel stopped reading. "I can't." His voice started to shake. "Will someone else?"

Greta was closest. She reached over, took the leather-bound book and began reading in a clear strong voice. When she began to fade, she passed it to another. The children took turns reading the rest of the afternoon and well into the evening. From beginning to end they heard every single word Daniel Rutherford Sutton had written for his eyes only. Zoë was the last one to read, closing with the reiteration of the words from hours before. When she finished they all just sat there, immersed in what they had read and overwhelmed by even more questions.

"Zoë, what are those?" Greta asked, indicating the bits of paper sticking out of the diary at various places.

"Oh, those are mine. I marked the ones that I thought might help us figure out what happened."

"Will you read those again?" Daniel asked, wiping his eyes unabashedly. Much of the diary had been about Daniel's mother, her illness and her slow death. It had been difficult for all of them to hear but Daniel insisted they read it, reminding them that the clue they needed could be anywhere.

Zoë cleared her throat and proceeded.

17 January 1958

Peri and I made some headway today in the lab. We're getting close, I can feel it. Bruiser says it's a lost cause and he wants us to work on something more profitable. The fool actually said "ladies' skin creams" to me. How he got a medical degree I'll never know. Still,

HC hasn't officially said "no" so Peri and I felt free to ignore him.

"I think 'HC' must be *Haverhill Chemicals*," Daniel added. "My grandfather worked there, remember? I wonder who 'Bruiser' is."

"We could ask Dr. Huntington. He's been there a long time. Maybe he knows," suggested Dinora.

"Maybe. It sounds like a nickname though, so he might not. Besides, if we asked, he might figure out we took the diary."

"If Peri was working with your grandfather," Greta began, "then he must have known Lionel too."

"Maybe he was Lionel and that was his code name," whispered Dinora, as she absentmindedly twirled her pigtail.

"But then he couldn't be Mr. P, though," said Seymour. "Mr. P was writing to Daniel ten years after Lionel was dead."

"True," agreed Dinora. "It is definitely difficult to be two people at the same time." She turned to Greta. "Believe me, I know."

Seymour chuckled quietly before encouraging, "Zo, will you read the next section?"

She scanned him for any trace of malice, found none and continued.

14 February 1958

We've done it! I still can't believe it. The world will never be the same and thank heaven for that. We still need to do the clinical trials to make sure but all evidence points to the fact that Peri and I are about to give humanity one heck of a Valentine's Day present.

I told Melonhead but he seemed more excited about the picture of the formula I drew for him. He also liked the ice cream I bought to celebrate. Little does he know. How I wish Gladys could be here for this. Still, my love, I know you're watching. Happy Valentine's Day.

"I wonder what the formula was," said Seymour.

"When he says 'the world will never be the same' it makes me think it was some kind of medicine," said Greta.

"Makes sense," said Daniel "*Haverhill Chemicals* makes all sorts of things—including medicine."

Zoë turned to the next marked page.

5 April 1958

Felicia has decided to stay on and I couldn't be happier. She seems tired more often lately and Melon is definitely a handful. It will be nice to keep them around. I've planted the wisteria outside her bedroom. It matches the paint perfectly and she was delighted. It's nice to see her smile again.

Bruiser keeps trying to pull us off the project—says the clinical trials are too expensive and HC believes they won't pan out. Sometimes I think they'd sell their souls if it could make them some money.

"Notice how this Bruiser keeps trying to keep them from working on the formula? That doesn't make sense to me," said Seymour. "If they were in the business of making medicine, why would he want them to stop?"

"It could be like this episode of *Mis Secretos* when Guillermo Marquez destroys the cure so that he can make even more money by selling medicine to all the sick people in the villages. But then his only daughter, Luisa, gets sick and dies. But it turns out that Luisa wasn't really his daughter but his *niece* because his wife had an affair with his brother, José Gabriel, who fought and died heroically in the—"

"Dinora," said Seymour.

"Oh, sorry. Sometimes I get carried away."

"It's okay," said Zoë. "Continue."

"Oh, that's pretty much it. Thank you, though. Read the next one."

Zoë shrugged and continued.

2 June 1958

I'm beginning to fear Felicia's symptoms are more than what they seem. Her fever last night peaked at 40° Celsius. Reggie came out but there wasn't much he could do that I hadn't already done. Still, when it's your little girl, you never quite see straight. Melon seems confused by it all. He doesn't understand why his mother can't play outside with him.

I haven't made it into the lab this week but Peri says that Bruiser has really stepped it up a notch. He thinks HC may even pull the plug on the project. Idiots, the lot of them.

Zoë saw Daniel's reaction and quickly skipped to the next entry.

The Diary

5 June 1958

It's confirmed. Felicia has the influenza. The irony. I've sterilized the house and taken Melon to stay with Dorothea. He wants desperately to see his mother and it breaks my heart not to let him. Still, it's for the best.

"So then Tia did know you, Danny. She took care of you when you were little."

"I'm so sorry about your mom," said Zoë, closing the book and passing it back to Daniel.

"Thanks."

"Daniel, may I see the diary for a second?" Greta asked. He passed it to her and she read part of the last section. "He says 'the irony'. I think the formula he found must have been something about the influenza."

"*The* influenza?" shouted Dinora. "The one that's killed hundreds of thousands of people all over the world?"

"Maybe they found a better medicine," said Zoë.

"But if that were true they wouldn't pull the plug on the clinical trials," said Seymour.

"It couldn't have been a medicine," said Greta. "He says 'the irony'. The only thing that would make it *ironic* would be if he developed a formula that would have prevented her from getting sick."

"You mean—" Daniel began.

"Yes," said Greta. "I think your grandfather developed a vaccine for one of the deadliest diseases of our generation."

22

∾ The Cinema ∾

Mr. Burl Dickson rifled quickly through the file, barely glancing at the paperwork. The children sat on the posh leather couch in the office of his impeccably-restored Victorian house.

"This should be no trouble at all," proclaimed the slightly-rotund litigator. He spoke as if he were addressing a jury. "This case is flim-flam—full of supposition but no actual admonition."

The children didn't say anything.

"It's rubbish," he clarified.

"Then you think you can do something?" asked Daniel excitedly.

"Think? I *know*, my boy. I'll call over to the courthouse this morning. See if we can't speak to a judge tomorrow, Wednesday at the latest."

"That's incredible! That's wonderful! Thank you so much, sir. Thank you!" Daniel pumped the large man's outstretched hand repeatedly, gushing with happiness.

"Happy to help," Mr. Dickson assured. "Now how can I reach you? You stay with Dorothea, am I right?"

"Yes but—"

"But you don't want your business known all over The Island?"

"Kind of," said Daniel sheepishly.

"Believe me, I know. I promise, when I call, I'll use all the discretion at my disposal. I'll call tomorrow with an update. Now you run along, enjoy the day. We'll have your grandfather out of there by the end of the week. At the latest!"

Daniel bounded out of the lawyer's office with the others in quick succession.

Zoë hung back and grabbed Seymour. "I think George is pulling some strings," she whispered.

"That's great. I hope he pulls every string he can. His friend is in jail. He's trying to help him out." He ran to catch up with the others. "Where to now?"

"*Cinema Magnifico!*" Dinora announced, flailing her arms dramatically.

When they arrived at the theater, the owner wasn't there.

"He'll be here later this afternoon though," said the man at the ticket counter. "Pop usually shows up around three or so."

"What to do until then?" asked Daniel.

"Let's watch the movie! Please, let's watch the movie!"

It was *Hello Dolly!* starring Dinora's most beloved American actress, Barbra Streisand. Since they needed to pass the time some way, and since Dinora was so very excited, they agreed. After Daniel had paid for the tickets, bought candy and popcorn, the five settled down for a relaxing afternoon. When it was over, they exited back into the plush foyer of the old theater.

"That must be the owner," Seymour said, indicating a man in a side office. He called out to him. "Sir?"

The man turned and squinted through thick black-framed glasses. "Oh, hello. You must be the lot my son told me about. I'm Mr. Petracelli. What can I do you for?"

"Sir, I know this might sound strange." Daniel carefully removed the small piece of faded red paper from his shirt pocket. He passed it to the man. "Does this mean anything to you?"

The man took the ticket stub and examined it closely. "Well I'll be. After all these years," he murmured to himself. He looked up at them. "You're definitely not what I expected but after this long it probably don't even matter. Here," he passed back the ticket stub. "Come in."

They crowded into the small office as the old man talked to himself. "I had it around here somewhere. Now where was it? Not there, not there. Where would I have put it?"

"What is 'it' exactly?" asked Daniel, fearful his anticipation would upset something but desperate to find out all the same.

"Hmm? Oh, an envelope," Mr. Petracelli answered absentmindedly. "It's definitely here somewhere."

"Is that it?" asked Greta. She had noticed a small white envelope, faded yellow with age, tacked to a bulletin board underneath a layer of other items the old man probably felt were important.

"Eh? Oh, will you look at that. So it is." He slowly made his way to the opposite wall, unpinned the envelope and set it in Daniel's eager hand. "I wondered when you'd come."

"What do you mean?" Daniel looked even more confused than usual.

"Long time ago, heavens now, must be nearly ten years, this fellow came by. He gives me a fiver and asks if I'll hold this envelope for a friend of his. He says someone will show up in the next few weeks and give me this here ticket stub. And when they do, I'm to give 'em the envelope." Mr. Petracelli shrugged his slightly-stooped shoulders. "Thing was, no one came. Every once in a while I'd wonder about it—wonder if I should open it up or just throw it out. Thinking maybe the fellow was just playing with me but he didn't seem the kind. Downright serious, respectable kind of chap."

"Sir?" Greta asked, reaching into her pocket and carefully removing a photograph. "Do you recognize this man here?"

Mr. Petracelli removed his glasses and held the picture away for a better look. "Why, that there's the scientist fellow. Gol' darn, if I can't remember his name."

"Daniel?" Daniel prompted.

"No, not Daniel," the man drawled and clicked his tongue. "Mind's not what it used to be. Anyhow, that's him. The scientist. Two of them, there were. Used to come every month. They loved the pictures, those two. Always came on the second night of the show—like clockwork. Said they didn't like the rush of the first day. New show'd start on the first, they'd be here on the second, sure as rain."

"Was there more than one showing?" Seymour asked.

"You bet—same as now. Got the matinee at one and the evening show at seven. Every day, 365 days a year since 1938," boasted Mr. Petracelli.

"Do you happen to remember what was playing?" asked Greta.

"Not off the top of my head, no, but I keep a record—along with audience numbers, that sort of thing." He walked over to a desk drowning in papers, but this time seemed to have no difficulty finding the thing for which he was looking. He opened up the grey, cloth-covered book and flipped back pages. "Here we are, second April 1959 was . . . *Anatomy of a Murder*." Mr. Petracelli released an audible sigh of reminiscence. "Jimmy Stewart was at the top of his game. And you know," he lectured, finger wagging, "if *Ben Hur* hadn't swept everything up, it would have won Best Picture. I'm sure of it. Course now, *Ben Hur*, that was a sight to behold. Eleven Oscars—first time in history and it's never been beat. Now *West Side Story*, she came close.

She took ten of 'em, but *Ben Hur*, now that was a film."
The man let out another wistful sigh. "Spectacular,
spec—" Mr. Petracelli froze in mid-sentence, a look of
realization dawning upon him.

"What is it?" Daniel asked urgently.

"Speck. Speck!" he said excitedly, snapping his
fingers to help him remember. "That was his name—or
something like it. And what was the other one—Perry!
Speck and Perry. *Specs*! That was it—on account of those
thick glasses he'd wear—called him Specs. Hmm," he
grunted.

"And did they both come that night?" asked
Seymour.

"Sure did but Perry, as I recall, left early. I remember
asking about it but he said something had come up and
he had to leave right away."

"He didn't say why?" asked Seymour.

"Not at all—only thing I could think of was that
he'd left the stove on. He and his brand-new *Mercury
Monterey* tore out of here in a hurry."

Greta's eyes lit up. She tugged on Seymour's jacket.
"Seymour, that's Lionel Robson's car."

Seymour looked confused. "How can that—are you
sure?"

"Absolutely. It was in the police report. Seymour,
Peri might be Lionel Robson."

"Then who is Mr. P?"

Daniel jerked his head in their direction, uncertain of
what he was overhearing. Whatever it was, he could learn
it later. Right now, he might just have the evidence he'd
been hoping for. "Mr. Petracelli, you're sure it was only
Peri who left early?" asked Daniel, his voice beginning to
quaver. "Sure it wasn't my—I mean, Specs?"

"Sure as can be. I'll never forget that night. You
don't walk out on Jimmy Stewart unless you think your
house might be afire."

"Mr. Petracelli, does it say in your book how long the movie was? When it would have gotten out?" asked Seymour.

"Sure does—let's see." He re-opened his book. "It was 160 minutes. Throw in about ten minutes of newsreels and advertising, I'd say folks would get out close to ten o'clock."

"The ferry schedule," whispered Greta.

"Sir, thank you so much for this." Daniel said. "You have no idea how much it means to us . . . to me."

"Well I'm not sure what I did but you're certainly welcome," replied Mr. Petracelli.

As they left the theater Daniel spoke first. "I don't have the schedule with me but I'd bet anything that the ferry my grandfather took was late enough to prove he couldn't have done it. That witness at the trial must have overheard someone else arguing with Lionel Robson—the real murderer."

"Yes!" said Greta. "The car crash was between nine and ten. Your grandfather has a solid alibi."

"Then that's it!" declared Seymour. "With Mr. Petracelli's testimony and the ferry schedule, we can prove he's innocent."

The children broke into a run, eager to secure some privacy on the open seas. Once they raised the mainsail Daniel began opening the envelope. Instantly, the rough wind snatched it out of his hands and hurled it up into the sails.

They all started screaming at once. Quick as a flash, Seymour leapt onto the cuddy cabin and launched himself into the sails, grasping the corner of the envelope between the very edges of his thumb and index finger. When his body slammed back down onto the boat, he cried out in pain.

"Seymour!" Zoë abandoned the helm and ran to her cousin.

With the absence of her captain, the boat lurched to the side. Thankfully Daniel was close enough to prevent further disaster. He wrestled with the helm until *The Prudence* was back under control and had stopped rocking precariously back and forth. A little sea water had gotten in, forcing each of them to remember how easily they could capsize if they didn't pay attention.

Tears of agony were streaming down Seymour's face and it looked to Daniel as if it were taking all the boy's energy not to completely lose control.

"I meant to learn first aid!" Now Dinora was crying. "After last summer—*sniff*—after Mario—I meant to learn first aid. Oh, why?" she wailed.

"Dinora!" Daniel barked, instantly getting the girl's attention and stopping her tears. "Take Greta below, now!"

Dinora looked at Greta, whose wan expression spoke volumes and whose eyes were staring straight ahead as if she had been transported into another world entirely—a watery world where she couldn't swim.

"Aye, aye!" Dinora shouted, whipping the small girl around and shoving her into the hull.

"Zoë, leave him! Help me turn the sail around."

Zoë didn't move.

Daniel screamed at her. "We can't help him with the boat like this. Now!"

She hesitated only a moment longer before letting Seymour's head fall and rushing to help Daniel. Together they warped *The Prudence* up into the breeze.

"Good," said Daniel. "Now get the first aid kit from below."

Zoë rushed off and Daniel went to Seymour, who now looked ready to faint. Expertly Daniel moved his hands around Seymour's leg.

"Zoë!" Daniel shouted. "Hurry up!"

Zoë emerged, holding the first aid kit and tripping in her desperation.

"Listen to me," said Daniel in a low sharp voice. "His knee has come out of its socket. I think I can put it back in but I need your help."

She nodded, using her sleeve to wipe the tears from her eyes.

"When I say 'go', I need you to pull his leg straight out as far as you can."

Zoë's face blanched. "But, but . . ."

"Zoë, you're just going to have to trust me. Are you ready?"

She nodded, although with considerably less confidence than before.

"Good." Daniel turned to his friend, who was now shaking with the pain. "Seymour, we're going to do something that is going to hurt a lot—for thirty seconds—and then the pain will be gone. I promise. When I say go—start counting. By the time you hit thirty, this will all be over. Ready?"

Seymour nodded with even less confidence than Zoë.

Daniel turned back to the girl next to him, "Like you've never pulled before—now!"

At his words Zoë began pulling, straightening Seymour's leg. Her cousin let out an anguished scream and in seconds Zoë's face was covered in tears, streaming from her eyes like a waterfall.

"Harder!" Daniel ordered and she pulled with all her might, causing even more pain.

Deftly, Daniel felt for the knee cap, placed the heel of his palm on one side, channeled all his strength and snapped it back in place.

There was a loud pop and then silence. Seymour's screaming stopped. Zoë's crying stopped. Daniel's breathing slowed and they all stared at Seymour's restored knee cap, each of them shocked it had actually worked.

"Daniel," said Seymour, struggling to calm himself. He held out his arms and Daniel leaned in for the huge boy's embrace. "Thank you."

Daniel laughed, releasing his own tension. "I'm just glad it worked. I knew how but I've never had to do it before."

"Danny," Dinora stood on the stairs, halfway up, with an awestruck look of unbounded proportions. "Where did you learn to do that?"

Daniel blushed and mumbled, "Edith's been teaching me some stuff."

"Like what?"

"Just stuff—you know—to take care of people."

"Danny, that was amazing."

"It really was," agreed Zoë.

"I'll say," said Seymour.

"How's Greta?" asked Daniel, anxious to change the topic.

"Oh, she passed out," explained Dinora calmly. "Probably for the best. Wow, Danny, I just . . . *wow.*"

"It's not over yet," he said. "Zoë, let's get *The Prudence* going. We need to get him to Doc Ingraham. Seymour, you're going to have to be pretty careful for at least a few weeks."

"Thank you, Daniel."

"I should thank *you*," said Daniel, nodding toward the envelope that the other boy still clutched in his hand. Seymour reached over and passed it to Daniel, who quickly folded it and returned it to the back pocket of his jeans. "We'll wait until we get back to Tia's."

23

❧ The Judge ❧

Daniel opened the envelope.

"A photograph of two men." He slipped out the matted paper and peered at it closely. "I think the one on the left is my grandfather."

"May I see?" asked Greta.

Daniel passed her the picture and she instantly recognized both men. "This is your grandfather." She looked up at him. "And he's standing with Lionel Robson."

Dinora and Zoë leaned in, nodding simultaneously. "Definitely," said Zoë. "Those are the men from the newspaper article we saw at the library."

"Then who is Mr. P?" Daniel wondered aloud before removing the remaining items—three pieces of paper.

"Those are from the diary!" said Greta, unaware she was practically shouting. She retrieved the old leather book, turned to the middle and examined it more closely. "Yes," she murmured, before looking up at a cadre of expectant faces. "There are pages missing but they're not torn out. They're—well, see for yourself." She passed the book to the others who inspected it in turn.

"Someone went to a fair amount of trouble to do that," she explained. "They would have to cut out the thread, remove the pages and sew it back together using the same holes as before. It would have taken a very long time." Greta set down the book. "The person who did this *wanted* someone to find the diary but wanted them to think it never included these entries." She carefully scanned the pages. "Listen," she said.

22 March 1959

I never thought I'd see the day when Peri would forsake humanity for money. In no way had I expected anything more from Bruiser—he's always had his own self-interests at heart. But Peri? HC made the offer today. Officially it wasn't an offer—they couldn't have their hands dirtied like that—but an offer, nonetheless. One million dollars.

To be sure, it's more money than Peri and I could spend in ten lifetimes but to what end? We have developed a vaccine against the worst disease in our lifetime and they want to bribe us to shut up about it so they can continue to milk people with their outrageously-overpriced medicines. It makes me sick. I hear Melon crying. That child is my only saving grace.

"Greta, you were right," exclaimed Dinora. "They did develop a vaccine."

"I wonder if George knew about it." Zoë tried to sound casual.

"There's no way," Daniel shot back. "He's a good man. If he'd known about this he would have done something."

"But George *worked* at *Haverhill*," she said desperately.

All were quiet and Greta resumed her reading.

25 March 1959

We're at a standstill. Peri wants to sign the contract and I refuse. Bruiser nearly lost control when I told him. For a second there, I thought he was going to hit me. Then he composed himself and said he understood and agreed with me but HC, they didn't see it that way and so on. Regardless, I fear the matter isn't resolved.

Technically, the formula belongs to HC but if they don't use it, I have no qualms about giving it to another company. It would serve them right. I have a nagging feeling this isn't the end of it, but I still can't believe anyone would do something rash. It's just money for heaven's sake.

"That's your proof right there!" Zoë screamed. "*Haverhill Chemicals* is run by a bunch of scumbags and George is at the top of the heap."

"Zoë," growled Seymour.

"Why am I the only one who sees this?"

"There's one more," said Greta, hoping to prevent another row between Zoë and any number of her friends.

1 April 1959

Apparently, we've entered a whole new realm of possibilities. How can human beings behave this way? My project is almost complete so at least I'll have that in case something happens. Melon has been helping me although I think he got more dirt on himself than anywhere else. He is so clever, that boy.

With this safety net in place, I suppose all I can do is wait and see how it all unravels. I'm sure HC will do the right thing in the end. How can they not?

"That's the last entry." Greta set down the papers.

"Maybe *Haverhill Chemicals* killed Lionel Robson and framed Danny's grandfather so they wouldn't tell people there was a vaccine," suggested Dinora in such a serene tone that the others were floored just as much by her demeanor as by the idea itself.

"I just can't believe that," said Daniel.

"Isn't that what your grandfather kept saying though?" Seymour asked. "Maybe we need to start thinking beyond the realms of belief too."

"But that's, that's—"

"Well, someone murdered him," argued Zoë. "He was in line for half a million dollars. I bet he was going to say 'yes' but your grandfather wouldn't agree and it wouldn't be of any use to ol' HC if it wasn't both of them who agreed to clam up."

Seymour considered this. "Then maybe they got nervous and decided to get rid of them. It would look suspicious if they both died, but if it appeared one killed the other it could wrap up into a tidy little solution."

"Plus, they'd save a million dollars," added Zoë wryly.

"You think they would do that? Just for the money?" asked Daniel.

"People have killed for less," said Seymour.

"And remember," Zoë added. "We're talking about *a ton* of money. Those medicines are expensive and a lot of people are sick. Remember in the article—"

"I have it!" Dinora reached for her yellow pad, which lately was never far from her, and read off the statistic. "In 1959, there were more than three million cases and 80,000 deaths—just in the United States alone."

Zoë was doing the math in her head. "Let's say the medicine is 50 dollars a person. At three million cases— that's 150 million dollars . . . a year. That means *Haverhill Chemicals* has made one and a half *billion* since it's been sitting on the vaccine."

"Not to mention the deaths of nearly a million people," added Greta's quiet voice.

"And that's just in the United States," said Dinora. "Who knows how many have died in the rest of the world." She paused before shouting, "We need to tell somebody!"

"Who would believe us?" said Zoë. "And what proof do we have—the diary of a murderer and a briefcase full of cash? That just makes *us* look guilty."

The phone rang and Daniel tore down the stairs. It wasn't long before he returned. "The judge said he'll see us tomorrow at noon. If the arguments are persuasive enough, he'll re-open the case."

The Belfast Courthouse loomed before them.

"I feel like Dorothy when she's about to meet the great and powerful Oz," whispered Dinora.

It was nearly noon and the four of them (Seymour was on crutches back at the house) were trying to decide if it was best to wait outside or enter.

"Well, there you are," said a familiar voice.

The children jumped, their attention so focused on the building they hadn't noticed Dr. Huntington approaching.

"Hello, Dr. Huntington! Isn't it a splendid day?"

"It sure is, Dinora. I'm glad to see you're in good spirits. But Danny, you seem nervous. Son, I tell you, everything is going to be just fine. Come now." He put an arm around Daniel and led the way.

Mr. Dickson had persuaded Judge Harold Haskell to meet with them during his lunch hour. When they arrived at the judge's chambers, the large man was just doffing his black robe, beneath which were the visible signs of his intention to golf that afternoon. He sat down heavily on a high-backed leather armchair and lit a cigar.

"Boys?" he offered the box to both Dr. Huntington and Mr. Dickson.

"No, Harry, 'fraid I can't. Millie says it's not good for me."

"These?" The judge looked incredulously at the cigar, which, now lit, was emitting a strong scent and clouds of smoke. "Nonsense. Nothing unhealthy about these. You got to be careful about girls like Millie, Burl. Don't let her forget who wears the pants in the family."

All three men laughed.

"Well, that may be true," Mr. Dickson paused as he reached into a paper bag and produced a package wrapped in tinfoil, "but she still makes the best lobster rolls in town."

"Oh bully!" The judge clapped his hands in delight and stubbed his cigar in the ashtray where it continued to smolder. "I was hoping you'd remember."

"Of course." Mr. Dickson winked at the kids. "Well, we sure appreciate you seeing us like this—on such short notice. Lunch is the least we can do."

"Well, any friend of Brewsy's is a friend of mine and I'm always happy to help out a friend. So what's the story?"

"Well, Your Honor," said Mr. Dickson in a more official tone. "We've come to ask you to reopen the case of *The People versus Daniel Rutherford Sutton*."

"Sutton, Sutton . . . isn't that the scientist fellow? Worked over with your folks at *Haverhill*?"

"Yes, Your Honor," said Dr. Huntington. "We believe he was falsely convicted."

"Murder as I recall. Nasty business that."

"Certainly, and just as nasty is that we put the wrong man in prison for the crime," said Mr. Dickson in an opening-statement kind of way.

"*If* that's the situation." cautioned the judge, before taking the last bite of his lobster roll and eyeing the paper bag next to Mr. Dickson's chair.

"That's what we'd like a chance to prove," responded the attorney. He reached into the bag and producing a second sandwich.

The judge licked his lips and chuckled again. "There's my boy!" He wasted no time starting in on the food. "Now reopening a case, that's tricky. The other judges don't like it when someone else messes with their business."

"That's why we came to you, Harry," said Dr. Huntington. "It was *your* case."

"Mine?" The judge looked surprised, then smiled. "No wonder it seems familiar. Well, seeing how it was mine, then I guess there's no harm in having another look. You being an old friend and all," he said to Dr. Huntington. "But boys—" Judge Haskell noticed the children for the first time. While the two men had taken seats in slightly-smaller armchairs facing the judge, the children had been relegated to a bench against the back wall. The judge lifted his chin grumpily in their direction. "What's with the *United Nations*?"

"You remember, Harry. I told you about Danny," said Dr. Huntington, motioning for Daniel to approach.

The boy hesitantly went to shake the judge's hand. "How do you do, sir?"

"Well enough, I suppose."

Dr. Huntington put his arm affectionately around Daniel's shoulders. "Harry, this is Sutton's grandson, named after him but goes by Danny." Beaming proudly he continued, "He's like a son to me."

This sentiment caught Daniel off guard but settled nicely. It felt good to belong to someone.

"Well I can see why you're so interested in having another look," said the judge, with an undertone Greta couldn't quite place. "Fair enough. I'll have my clerk clear some time tomorrow."

"Thank you, Your Honor!" said Daniel earnestly.

"Thanks, Harry," added Dr. Huntington. "I owe you one."

"Your Honor," said Mr. Dickson, glancing quickly at Dr. Huntington. "You'll also need to ask your clerk to arrange for the prisoner to be brought."

"What's that? No need for that. Highly irregular that. We'll see if your argument holds any water. If it does, we can bring him in then."

"Harry," said Dr. Huntington, a little forcefully. "We've reason to believe that it's the prisoner himself who has information vital to proving his innocence."

"Actually, we found—" began Daniel.

"Son," Dr. Huntington said tersely. "Let me handle this."

Daniel looked confused.

The eyes of the two men locked for a moment and Greta noticed a subtle hand gesture where Dr. Huntington seemed to flick some particle off his breast pocket. *He keeps his wallet there*, she thought.

Judge Haskell's expression darkened momentarily but was quickly replaced with a smile. "Well, I suppose it couldn't hurt," he said hesitantly, then apparently warmed to the idea. "Very well, I'll speak to Forest about it, see what we can do."

"You're the best, Harry." Dr. Huntington shook his hand before turning to corral the children out of the office.

"What did you mean in there?" asked Daniel as they exited the courthouse. "About my grandfather having information."

"Oh, nothing in particular. I guess I told a little white lie just then. Truth is, when we prove him innocent, I want him to be able to walk right out of that courtroom and home with us. He's been caged up far too long. I couldn't bear it another instant."

24

❧ The Hearing ❦

The next twenty-four hours passed with excruciating slowness and by the next morning, all of the children were little more than bundles of frayed nerves.

"I think we should call Dr. Huntington," said Daniel.

No one dared disagree, even though all along Daniel had been the one insistent on being discreet. Discretion had now given way to desperation and Daniel scrambled to find the business card that lay on the library table along with the other assembled evidence. As he grabbed it, a few of the lighter items fell to the floor, including the photograph of the two scientists.

"I'll be right back," he said, racing out of the room.

Greta went to pick up the fallen items and as she did she took a closer look at the photograph that had been enclosed in the envelope left at *Cinema Magnífico*.

"Do you see something?" asked Seymour, who was resting his leg on the ottoman.

She didn't answer. Instead she took the picture over to an antique magnifying glass in the corner. "Aha!" she cried.

"Aah!" screamed Dinora, who was the most on edge of the children.

"Get a grip, girl," scolded Zoë. "What is it, Greta?"

"It's proof. It's solid proof he couldn't have done it."

The other two girls rushed to join her.

"How?" asked Seymour, reaching for his crutches and struggling to stand. "I thought it was just a picture of the two of them."

"So did I, but come look where they are," said Greta.

"It's the *Cinema Magnifico*!" cried Dinora. "But that still doesn't tell us the date and time.

"Yes it does!" Greta said excitedly. "Look, there's the clock on the town hall. It's a little before seven—right before they caught the evening show."

Dinora began jumping up and down. "With Mr. Petracelli's testimony this is sure to be enough!"

"Not necessarily," said Zoë. "They could always argue about the date."

Greta shook her head. "Look at what Lionel Robson is holding."

Dinora stopped jumping to peer more closely. "It's a newspaper."

"Hey!" shouted Zoë.

"What is it?" shouted Seymour, still trying to make his way from the other end of the room.

Zoë brought the paper to him. "Under the magnifying glass you can see the date. It's April 2nd. The night of the murder. He's holding it perfectly."

"Danny! We've got wonderful news!" greeted Dinora as the door opened. "Danny? Are you okay?"

"Yeah, I'm fine. I just spoke with Dr. Huntington. He said the judge is going to use the courtroom in Deer Isle. They're coming now. With my grandfather. Here. Now."

"Hooray!" they shouted.

"We'll drive down and meet them," said Seymour.

The others looked at his leg.

"I don't know what it is you're looking at but there is no way I'm missing this," he said haughtily.

Within the hour they were pulling up in front of the courthouse. Directly in front of them was a police car. An officer was holding the door open for an old man in handcuffs.

Dinora gasped. "Danny, is *that* your grandfather?"

Daniel nodded.

"He's so old. I can't believe he and Dr. Huntington were classmates."

Daniel ignored her. "Grandfather?" he called.

The older man didn't turn but the officer did. "Kid, your grandpa's in our custody. You need to keep your distance."

Daniel watched as they went into the back entrance of the courthouse. "Let's go," he told the others.

With Seymour on crutches, they slowly followed.

Dr. Huntington was waiting for them, visibly agitated. "Danny, you didn't tell me about your grandfather. Why didn't you tell me?"

"What do you mean?"

"You know very well what I mean. Is he even in his right mind?"

"You said you didn't need him, that you had your own evidence."

"I didn't know he was a walking vegetable!" Dr. Huntington nearly shouted.

The look on Daniel's face and the turning heads around them brought back Dr. Huntington's self-control. "Danny, how long has he been like this?" His voice was calmer now and it was clear how much he cared for his friend.

Daniel imagined how devastating it must be for Dr. Huntington to find out only now what Daniel himself had known for weeks.

"I'm sorry," Daniel apologized. "I should have told you. He's been like that ever since I began visiting him. I don't know if it's permanent but I . . . I hope not."

"So then what have you talked about with him?" asked Dr. Huntington, putting his arm around Daniel and leading him into the courtroom, away from the others.

"Nothing, really. He doesn't even recognize me or know who I am."

"I see."

Zoë turned to face her friends, her arms outstretched toward Dr. Huntington and Daniel. "Now do you—"

"Zoë, how can you be so cruel? Just let them be, okay? Can't you see how much they're hurting?" Seymour said.

"You have got to be kidding me!" Zoë turned on her heel and marched into the near-empty courtroom.

"And it starts again," sighed Seymour, heading after her.

Greta and Dinora followed.

"All rise," instructed the bailiff in a booming voice. "This is a hearing to review the status of *The People versus Daniel Rutherford Sutton*. The Honorable Judge Harold Haskell presiding."

The judge sat, hammered his gavel and cleared his throat impatiently. "Well, we're here to question the man. Let's get him out here."

The bailiff went to a door and spoke quickly with a court official. Greta shuddered with emotion as, within moments, the once-brilliant scientist who had helped discover the vaccine with the potential for saving millions of lives, had his handcuffs removed and was escorted to the stand.

Another court officer brought a small black bible forward. "Place your left hand here and raise your right," he instructed.

The old man looked at him and turned to survey the courtroom. His eyes rested on the spot where Daniel sat with Dr. Huntington. He squinted in what seemed to be a look of recognition. Slowly, he raised his hand.

"Do you solemnly swear that what you are about to say is the truth, the whole truth and nothing but the truth, so help you God?"

The prisoner slowly shook his head. The other man turned to the judge for direction.

"Sir?" the judge called. "Mr. Sutton, sir, you must take the oath before taking the stand."

"Taking?" the old man asked hoarsely. "Taking? Taking, taking . . . they're taking my Melon. They're taken my Melon! Melon!"

"Good God, man, get a hold of yourself!" shouted Judge Haskell.

But Mr. Sutton only became more belligerent. He made an angry dash toward Daniel but Greta noticed it was Dr. Huntington who flinched.

Instantly, the bailiff apprehended the prisoner and replaced the handcuffs.

"Bailiff, take him away at once," roared the judge.

Mr. Sutton started screaming for his grandson as the bailiff tried to guide him away.

"Danny, did you know about this?" Dr. Huntington asked tightly.

"Yes, sir," answered Daniel.

The judge slammed his gavel. "Well, counselor. Your first plan of attack didn't seem to work so unless you've brought me out here to waste my time I suggest you get on with it."

"Of course, Your Honor," Mr. Dickson agreed, casting an open and questioning look at Dr. Huntington.

Greta was watching Dr. Huntington carefully and what she saw next was so subtle she wasn't even sure if it was true. *It looks like he just shook his head—but ever so slightly*, she thought.

Perhaps she was right, for Mr. Dickson didn't seem at a loss now. "Unfortunately, Your Honor, I'm afraid our case was resting on the testimony of Mr. Sutton himself."

"But you said—" Daniel turned accusingly to Dr. Huntington.

"Order in the court!" Judge Haskell bellowed, banging his gavel repeatedly. "This is highly irregular."

"Your Honor, we have evidence!" shouted Seymour.

"Eh? What's that? Who are you? This is highly irregular."

Wincing a little, Seymour stood. "Your Honor, we have proof that Mr. Sutton was off The Island when Lionel Robson died."

"What is this proof?" asked the judge.

"Yes, what is it?" asked Dr. Huntington eagerly. "Danny, why didn't you tell me you had proof? Son, this is wonderful news! Where is it?"

"Your Honor," interrupted Mr. Dickson. "May it please the court, might we have a short recess to gather the evidence?"

"I haven't got all day, Burly," snarled the judge.

"It won't take long," Daniel pleaded. "I can be back within the hour." He saw the man hesitating. "You could have lunch at *Mandy's*."

Judge Haskell considered this. "Well, a man does need to eat. Very well but if you're not back by—" he glanced at his large expensive watch, "—one o'clock, I'm leaving and this case is closed. Permanently."

"Yes, sir. I'll—" began Daniel.

"MELON!" came the blood-curdling scream from behind closed doors. "Where's my Melon?"

Daniel's face blanched. He turned to Seymour, helplessly. "Seymour, will you?"

Seymour looked at his leg. "I can try," he said doubtfully.

"I'll drive up there, Danny!" Dinora offered.

"Danny, don't worry a second more," comforted Dr. Huntington. "I'll drive up there and get it. That way you can stay with your grandfather. That's all right, isn't it Harry? If the boy stays with his grandfather?"

Judge Haskell looked as if he thought it wasn't one bit "all right" but didn't particularly want to say so. "It's not exactly procedure. But, uh . . . seeing as how they're related—"

"Wonderful. Danny, the bailiff here will take you to him. See if you can't calm his nerves, poor soul. Just tell me where to find the—"

"Not so fast, mister," interrupted Zoë. "You leave that part to me. All you need to do is drive." She marched off toward his convertible, parked in front of the courthouse.

Dr. Huntington stood there, seething in irritation. But in mere seconds the redness had vanished from his face and the whiteness from his knuckles. His skin resumed its golden tones and his blue eyes held no trace of the fury Greta was certain she'd just seen. He laughed. "Very well," he said. "We'll be back in a jiffy."

Judge Haskell stepped down from the bench and removed his robe. "Remember the lemon meringue pie, Burly? You think it's still as good as when we were in high school?"

"I'm sure it is, Harry," Mr. Dickson answered, escorting the judge out of the building. The former classmates seemed much more moved by the idea of lunch than the fact that a man's future lay in a precarious balance.

"There's our justice system for you," scoffed Seymour dejectedly.

"It's not fair," said Dinora. "But Zoë will get the picture and this afternoon Danny will have his grandfather back . . . and then they'll move in with Dr. Huntington and we'll probably never see Danny again and then if my knee becomes dislocated I'll just sit there in agony—like Consuela in *Mis Secretos* when she is trying to escape from Juan Humberto and she falls down the stone steps and twists her ankle and can't run and he just looks down at her, laughing and laughing until the commercial."

The Hearing

"Greta?" Seymour asked. "You okay?"

"High school!" she cried. "The yearbook!"

Understandably, the others looked confused.

Hastily, she explained. "The night we arrived, I was reading books in Tia's library and I found a yearbook—from *Deer Isle High School*. It was from a long time ago but there was *something* about it."

"The library should have the old yearbooks," said Seymour. "We have an hour. Let's check it out."

"We *could* have lunch," Dinora began but quickly followed with, "but probably looking at old books makes more sense."

Slowly, Seymour struggling with his crutches, the children made their way to the library at the other end of town, where they were greeted warmly by Miss Emma Darling. She immediately directed them to a section on the second floor. "Here they are," she announced proudly. "All the way back to 1897 when the school was founded."

"Where should we start?" Seymour asked Greta.

"How old do you think he is?"

"Danny's grandfather?" asked Dinora. "He looks about a hundred, maybe more."

"Why don't we start with 1915?" suggested Seymour. "We can check the class lists. Are we looking for his year?"

Greta considered this. "I'm not sure exactly. There's just something about how it was written—like in the seniors' section. It could be nothing, but maybe not. I think it might be something." She was trying to keep panic at bay. "I think it might be something important." She passed *1915* to Seymour, *1916* to Dinora and took *1917* for herself.

They worked diligently. After about ten minutes, Seymour declared. "Nothing. If he wasn't even a freshman in 1915, then that would rule out the next three years. Greta, will you pass me *1919*?"

She did so and passed Dinora *1923*. She thought of how old Mr. Sutton *did* look and decided to check *1911* for good measure.

"I found him!" shouted Seymour, earning an expert shush from below. "He was a freshman in 1919 so he graduated in 1922."

Greta promptly retrieved the book and made her way to a nearby table. Seymour hobbled over, sat down and the girls leaned in on either side of him as he opened to the first page.

"Oh look, it's Dr. Huntington," fawned Dinora. "Doesn't he look handsome in his football uniform?" They turned a few more pages. "Oh, and here he is at the Winter Dance. I bet he was quite a catch!"

Four more pages and they saw their first picture of Mr. Sutton. "The Science Club," Seymour read. "That's Daniel's grandfather. I'm sure of it. Look at those glasses."

"And that's Lionel Robson to his left. They look like best friends," said Dinora sadly.

The next page held another picture of Dr. Huntington with a group of students and a few pages after that, even more.

"There sure are a lot of pictures of him," commented Seymour.

"He looks like the most popular kid in school and yet he was best friends with . . . well, someone who probably wasn't as popular," whispered Dinora discretely. "Even back then he cared about people."

Greta brought the book closer. "But if they were best friends, why aren't there any pictures of them together?" She began flipping through the pages. "Look." She pointed to the page, then turned another. "And here . . . and here. All of these pictures focus on Dr. Huntington. Daniel's grandfather is nowhere in sight. Except this one—it looks like it was some sort of picnic or celebration—all three are in the same picture but Dr. Huntington couldn't be farther from the other two."

"Maybe they were in a fight that day," suggested Dinora.

Greta didn't respond. She went to the section which held the individual pictures of the graduating class. She found Lionel Robson first. "Here it is," she said, reading aloud. "Lionel James Robson. Science Course. 'His studious nature is sure to bring him his goal of adding an element to the Periodic Table.' Hmm. I wonder if that's where he got his nickname from." Greta scanned the next page. "And here's Daniel's grandfather. Daniel Rutherford Sutton. Science Course. Voted most likely to win a Nobel Prize. 'Laughs lots—when in the right crowd. Specs spends his free time gardening.' Oh, my." Clearly panicked, Greta began flipping the pages in the opposite direction.

"What is it?" asked Seymour.

"I want to check something." She found the page and traced her shaking finger along it. "Here he is, George Tyler Huntington . . . oh no."

"What?" the other two asked in unison.

"Oh my . . . oh my," Greta began to hyperventilate.

Seymour grabbed the book from her. Dinora peered over his shoulder. They both found it at the same time.

George Tyler Huntington
Normal Course
Athletic Editor; Captain D.I.H.S. football
"Bruiser is the man to follow."

25

❧ The Discovery ❧

Zoë stewed in the passenger seat and Dr. Huntington made no effort at small talk. The twenty-minute ride was shortened by his speedy and reckless driving. However the tension counteracted this effect and the trip still lasted much longer than either would have liked.

They pulled into the long driveway leading up to Tia's house.

Before the car was completely stopped, Zoë opened her door and hopped out. "I'll be right back." She pointed her index finger right in his face. "You stay here."

She rushed into the house calling loudly, "Tia, Edith, I'm back!" This was mostly for Dr. Huntington's benefit. She wanted him to believe there were adults nearby. She also secretly hoped the two women had returned from their "errand" because she could really use a little adult supervision right about now.

Zoë didn't risk calling a second time as this might alert Dr. Huntington to the fact that the adult residents might not be at home. For a moment she considered faking Tia's voice but wasn't entirely sure she could pull it off.

As she was puzzling through all of this, she was making her way up to the library, two steps at a time. When she found the box, she rifled through it. *What to take*, she wondered. Deciding against the baby stuff and the key, Zoë gathered the diary (including the missing pages), the ticket stub and the photograph from the movie theater. She tore down the stairs, through the living and dining rooms, into the spacious kitchen and right smack into George Tyler Huntington.

Zoë reeled back from the impact. "*You*! I told you to stay in the car!"

Dr. Huntington smiled, flashing his perfect white teeth. "I was worried about you," he mocked. "It's a big house. I didn't want you to get lost without anyone here to help you find your way back."

"I knew you were up to something!"

"And so I was. Yet none of your friends believed you." He shook his head in fake sympathy. "Not even your own cousin. What a shame. Must have made you feel like a pesky . . . insolent . . . insignificant . . ." With each word the older man was easing forward, reaching for her. "Worthless . . . little . . . brat!" He lunged for her and Zoë dodged behind the kitchen island situated in the exact center of the room.

"I knew it! I knew it! I knew you weren't who you said you were!" she screamed.

"And you were right and no one believed you. How sad for the little baby."

"You probably don't even believe he's innocent!"

"I don't *care* if he killed Peri or not. The old fool has gone completely mad. He doesn't even know his own grandson and that's all the information I need," he growled, continuing to circle the island with her on the opposite side—like a cat and mouse. *And I'm the mouse*, thought Zoë, racking her brain for options.

"Look, missy, you and I both know there is no way out for you. You can keep up your little game of 'ring around the rosy' as long as you like. It's nearly one o'clock now. Even if we left this minute we'd barely make it in time. So the longer you keep it up, the better for me. In a few minutes, none of your evidence will matter." He nodded toward the items clutched in her hand and his eyes caught the diary. "You little thief! You took that from my office!"

"Talk about the pot calling the kettle black! We know exactly what you were up to over there at your fancy *Haverhill Chemicals*. We know all about the vaccine and how you tried to cover it up. We know you are the ones who really killed Lionel Robson."

"That's quite an accusation, young lady."

"We just don't have a way to prove it! But we *do* have enough to prove Daniel's grandfather didn't," she said, waving the contents of her hand at him threateningly.

"Is that so? Like what?"

Is he nervous? Zoë wasn't able to see through his well-practiced façade. "Like an iron-tight alibi! He was at the movies that night. We have an eye-witness and everything. There's no way he could have done it."

"Eye-witnesses only get you so far," he warned in a smooth, tightly-controlled voice.

"Yeah? And what about photographs?" She waved the picture in front of Dr. Huntington's face—taunting him. "This here is a picture of him with Lionel Robson! He's alive, by the way, so it was before your goons got to him."

"What do I care about a picture?"

Yes, she thought, *he is nervous*. "You'd care if you knew it was taken the night of the murder, right before the show."

"Oh, and I suppose there just *happens* to be a date and time on the picture?" he asked, derisively.

"As a matter of fact there is. The town hall clock and the daily paper, so there!" She shouted this last bit as she reached for a jar of kitchen utensils and flung it at Dr. Huntington. She had re-positioned herself and now she had her back to the side entrance. It was to this door that she ran and swung open. Or at least tried. She grabbed the handle but the door wouldn't budge. She shook it mightily and Dr. Huntington started laughing. She turned to him. Regular tennis matches had honed his reflexes and kept him in great shape. He had easily ducked, leaving the large glass container she'd thrown to shatter unobstructed on Tia's stone floor.

In no time at all he was upon her, shoving her against the door and twisting her arm behind her.

Zoë screamed in pain.

"I locked it, you dim-witted twit!" Dr. Huntington laughed again.

Zoë cursed herself for her own stupidity. Tia never locked the doors. No one on The Island did. She didn't even know the door *had* a lock. She glanced upward and saw the cast-iron sliding bolt.

"I'll take those," grunted Dr. Huntington, further pressuring her wrist so she had no choice but to let go. He tucked the diary and papers behind the small of his back.

Zoë took advantage of the movement to wrench free of his grasp and make a dash for safety. The first door she found was to the larder. It swung open easily. She darted inside and slammed the door shut, clinging to the handle with all her might and hoping it would be enough to fend him off. "Try and hurt me now, you greedy scum-bucket!" she screamed, desperate to think of a way to get the evidence back.

"Hurt you? What do you take me for?" Dr. Huntington asked coolly. "I wouldn't think of it."

Zoë could hear the sound of wood scraping against stone. *He's dragging something,* she thought. The sound was getting louder. *A chair?*

"In fact, you couldn't have placed yourself more perfectly. Finally, you managed to do something helpful."

Zoë felt the door handle jiggle. She renewed her determination not to let him in. Then she realized what was happening. She relaxed her hold. Nothing. She turned the handle. Still nothing. She pushed to open the door. Nothing. She was trapped. "You jerk! Let me out of here."

"Now if you're just going to use foul language—"

"Let—me—out!" she shrieked, accentuating each word by banging on the wooden door.

"Your parents really were remiss in not teaching you better manners."

"Oh yeah? Well your parents were *remiss* in sending you to charm school! They should have taught *you* how to be a decent human being! Now you're just a low-down dirty crook with fancy—" Zoë heard a click and a crinkling sound. "What are you doing?"

"Oh, let's just say I'm tidying up. There are a few loose ends out here."

It's a lighter. "You can't burn those! Please!" she implored. "That's all we have. Please! It doesn't even matter to you if he goes free. You don't care. You said so yourself. Please! I'm sorry, I'm so sorry I was rude. It's good you went to charm school. You're not that much of a crook and . . . and . . . Dr. Huntington? Dr. Huntington?"

She wasn't sure how much time had elapsed, but her voice had long been hoarse from screaming. It was definitely past one o'clock, probably even two by now. Had the judge left? What must Daniel be thinking of her? She pictured Dr. Huntington cruising along in his baby blue convertible, laughing maniacally at the fools he had made of all of them. *Especially me.*

"Hello?" came a southern-accented voice from the hallway. It was just about the sweetest sound she'd ever heard.

"Hello!" shouted Zoë, as best she was able.

Slow footsteps made their way toward her. "The door was open and I . . . might Miss Witherspoon be at home?"

"Will you let me out, please?"

There was a shove and a scrape and Zoë opened the door. "Thank you, Mr. Billings."

"Are you all right, miss?"

"Me? Oh, yeah. I'm fine. But we need to go now!"

"But is Miss Witherspoon—"

"She's not here. C'mon Billings, there's no time to waste."

He quickened his step to keep up with her. She jumped into the front of the black Rolls Royce and turned to the chauffeur. "Put the pedal to the metal, my man!"

Once they had discovered Dr. Huntington's identity, Seymour and the girls frantically returned to the courthouse. After an infuriatingly long time they were able to retrieve Daniel and tell him what they'd learned.

"Zoe!" shouted Seymour in the middle of their explanation, just realizing his cousin might be in danger.

An immediate look of understanding came across the others' faces.

"I'll drive," Daniel said gruffly.

"Thanks, Daniel," said Seymour, glancing at his watch. "I'll try to buy some more time with the judge."

The others rushed to the truck and sped out of town.

"Oh dear. Oh no. Oh dear. Oh no," repeated Dinora for the first five minutes.

"Dinora, please," Daniel said tightly.

"Oh, sorry. Oh dear, oh—" Dinora muzzled her mouth with her hand for the remainder of the ride.

As they turned onto Tia's driveway they were nearly hit head-on by a shiny Rolls Royce, which skidded to a halt. Zoë jumped out and told them her news.

"All of it?" asked Daniel desperately. "You're sure?"

"I'm sorry, Daniel. It's gone."

Upon hearing this, all hope drained from the boy's face. "Then it's over," he said, expressionless. Everything and everyone froze. Time seemed to stand still as the information consumed him. All of their work—the clues, The House, the box, finding the truth about his mother, reuniting with a grandfather he didn't even remember and now realized he loved regardless. All of it, over. His grandfather would go back to prison. Forever.

Slowly, Daniel turned the Chevy around. Zoë climbed into the truck bed and hugged her knees to her chest. The children made their way back to town in sorrow and in silence.

Seymour greeted them. "The judge stayed," he said excitedly. When this didn't garner the expected reaction, he asked, "What's wrong?"

"Dr. Huntington destroyed the evidence," answered Greta. "All of it."

Daniel sat, devastated, on the courthouse steps. The others sat with him, in solidarity, but none spoke. What was there to say? No amount of comforting could ease this kind of heartbreak.

"He's all I have," said Daniel, flatly. "He doesn't even know I exist but . . . he's all I have."

Dinora put her arm around him but even that seemed of such little use it hardly mattered. Daniel stared blankly ahead, lost in despair.

No one suggested anything. Their evidence was gone. Mr. Dickson and Dr. Huntington were nowhere in sight.

"We could try talking to the judge ourselves," said Greta. "You never know."

Daniel didn't bother to respond and even Dinora, easily the most optimistic of the bunch, had sensed the judge's motives didn't particularly derive from a sense of justice.

"It's at least worth a try," said Seymour, using his crutches to help him stand.

The five children returned to the courtroom, saw it was empty and made their way to what they assumed were the judge's chambers. They knocked on the door.

There was no response.

"I bet he's sleeping off lunch," whispered Dinora as she took the liberty of pounding hard enough to wake the dead.

They heard grunts and movement from within, then a command. "Enter."

Seymour turned the doorknob and pushed open the door. "Excuse me, Your Honor," he said.

"Oh, it's you," said Judge Haskell, disappointed. His white hair skewed to the left from his nap. "Am I to presume you've returned with this so-called 'incontrovertible evidence'?"

Seymour braced himself for an uphill battle. "Your Honor, the evidence has been destroyed but—"

"Destroyed? Highly irregular. By whom?"

"By a scoundrel who goes by the name of George Tyler Huntington!" trumpeted Dinora.

"Brewsy? Hardly the chap to meddle in that sort of nonsense. No, you must be mistaken."

"But he—" began Dinora, before Seymour put an arm on her shoulder to stop her.

"Your Honor, we have an eye-witness who can swear to seeing the defendant on the night of the murder. There's no way he could have killed Lionel Robson."

The judge looked perturbed. "And where's your law degree, son?"

"I don't, but I—"

"I thought not. No, you children run along now. Justice was served ten years ago and my time has been wasted too much already."

"But that's not fair!" shouted Zoë.

"Bailiff!" boomed the judge. "Remove these children at once!"

The door opened, but instead of the short, red-faced bailiff, it was a tall man with black hair slicked to the sides.

"*The man,*" whispered Greta, and the other children too had recognized him at once as the man from the café.

"What's this? You're not my bailiff."

"No, Your Honor, but I do represent someone who has information vital to this case."

"I've had enough of this case! Bailiff!"

"Your Honor, you would be well-advised to hear out my client."

"Bailiff! Where is that fool? Oh, lunch. Well get on with it, then."

"Your Honor, it would be best if you spoke with him in private." The man eyed the children.

"We've every right to hear what you have to say!" shouted Dinora.

"Oh, pipe down, child, before I have you taken into custody. Go on, man, tell me how you're so certain Daniel Sutton didn't kill Lionel Robson."

A voice came from the doorway. "Because *I* am Lionel Robson."

They all stood and stared, mouths gaping wide as a shorter man stepped through the doorway. The first man moved aside to make way for him.

"Well, so you are. I'll be," mumbled a dazed Judge Haskell.

"You'll be many things, Harry," said the cool voice of a man very much alive. "But the first thing you'll do is release Dr. Sutton."

The bailiff rushed in at that point, his napkin still sticking out of his collar. "You called, Your Honor?"

The judge simply stared. "Yes, I, well, I hardly . . . these things need to be done in proper order. There are forms and such."

"My associate here," Mr. Robson nodded toward the tall serious man, "will go with your bailiff to take care of all the formalities. In regards to letting him go, there is no question. You can hardly hold a man for killing another man who happens to be standing in your office at this very moment."

Judge Haskell seemed at a loss for words.

Mr. Robson reached for his wallet and continued. "I am very willing to take care of any other *business*—or questions—once we are alone."

Judge Haskell became quite interested in putting all of this unpleasantness behind him. "Bailiff, make arrangements to release the prisoner at once."

The bailiff turned and left. The tall man motioned for the children to follow. Daniel's gaze shifted from one man to the next to the third.

"Danny, let's go. He's free," a familiar voice next to him urged.

He let himself be guided out of the room and down a hall. He stood next to a counter while the guard unlocked a cell, then handcuffs and then . . . there he was, his grandfather.

Daniel began to cry.

Miss Dorothea Witherspoon didn't say a word as the children began spilling out the whole story in all its dramatic detail. And although her lips didn't move, the rest of her was quite busy. As soon as she saw the bewildered scientist walk into her home she took matters into her own hands. She sat them all down at the large oak table in her kitchen, where she began preparing every possible form of culinary comfort. First, hot tea—for Dr. Sutton. Then, a small sandwich and a cup of soup—for Dr. Sutton. After which, some blueberry pie with a skosh of ice cream—for Dr. Sutton. Once these duties had been dispatched, she fed the rest of them.

Of course none of the children minded this at all. If there was anything they could do for Daniel's grandfather, they were happy to do it.

"Seymour, in the boys' closet you should find some clothes for Dr. Sutton. Zoë, will you prepare the room next to Daniel's. Make up both beds as Daniel will feel more comfortable if he's close to his grandfather." Her orders given, Tia returned to the story. "Forgive me, my darlings, please continue. You were telling me of Mr. Petracelli."

Dinora continued, with occasional contributions (or clarifications) from Greta, until finally the whole story had been told. Tia eyed Daniel but didn't ask once about why he hadn't wanted to tell her about his grandfather. Dorothea was not one to speculate.

Two pairs of feet stomped down the kitchen stairs. "The room is all ready, Daniel," said Zoë, who had shown surprising graciousness by not saying, "I told you so" *too* many times.

"I put clothes for your grandfather in the bureau and a new toothbrush in the bathroom," added Seymour.

"Thank you," said the boy, whose mind was clearly still reeling from all that had happened so very quickly. "I think we'll go up then." He stood and put his arms on his grandfather's shoulders. "Grandfather, I'll take you upstairs now."

"Upstairs? Is that you, Melon?"

The Discovery

A fresh batch of tears appeared on the boy's face. "Yes, grandfather. It's Melon," he choked back a sob. "I'm here and everything is going to be okay."

26

✤ The Proposal ✦

By the end of the third week everyone had adjusted to the new routine. Tia and Daniel took care of Dr. Sutton, helping him acclimate to life outside of prison.

Dr. Ingraham said it would take awhile before they could figure out how much of the dementia was reversible. "He's in poor health but a few months with Dorothea will take care of that." He removed his cap and scratched his head. "As far as the rest, Danny, I think we're just going to have to wait and see."

Sensing they would be in the way around the house, the others enlisted Edith's help on a project of their own. It proved to be the perfect distraction and the children excitedly jumped out of bed each morning, ate a full breakfast and packed enough food to feed an army. By dinnertime, they were dirty and exhausted but had nothing of great importance to share on how they were spending their days. When Tia did ask Edith about it, the woman simply responded, "Well, since they're not breaking into local businesses, I wouldn't worry too much about it."

The Proposal

One beautiful Sunday evening, still early enough for the sun to stroke the hayfields around the large house, Daniel and his grandfather were just returning from a walk around the orchard—one of the daily activities that seemed to help both the old man's muscles and his memory. It looked so enjoyable in fact that Tia asked Edith, "Darling, shall we take a little evening constitutional ourselves?"

Edith looked up from the strange mechanical object she appeared to be either building or dismantling. "That sounds nice, Dot."

Arm in arm, the two women strolled out past the orchard to the bluff overlooking the Atlantic Ocean.

The children and Dr. Sutton were in the library, where they tended to spend their evenings in various solitary pursuits, when not engaged in the music room. Daniel had taken to giving his grandfather different reading materials in case something might trigger a memory or a reaction of any sort. So far, none of the books had been effective. The man simply let them sit in his lap as he stared out the window.

Zoë and Greta would work on their Mandarin lessons, unless Zoë was playing chess with Seymour, in which case Greta had found another occupation. She was attempting to reconstruct the diary from memory—especially those missing pages.

"Remember, how he had his 'project' just in case? I'm sure that's the formula. If we can figure that out—we might still have a chance of getting it into the hands of people who can do something with it."

"He mentioned you helping, Danny. Do you remember anything?" asked Dinora.

"If there was a project, it would have been destroyed long ago with everything else in The House. I don't mean to be rude and you know how much I'd love to find the formula, but right now I need to figure out a place to stay and a means of supporting us."

"You're not just going to stay here?" asked Seymour.

"I can't depend on Tia forever. That's not fair to her and she's already been so kind to me. Then again, it's not as if I had another place to stay." He stared dejectedly out the window, mirroring his grandfather.

"That's not true, Daniel," said Greta. "You have your house."

"I'm never going there again," he said bitterly. "I hate that place."

The children exchanged furtive glances.

"Then where will you stay, Danny?" asked Dinora.

"I guess here for the time being. I know Tia would never kick us out but it's not right. I have my college money but that won't last us very long. And I can't take care of my grandfather and work and go to school."

"Why don't you just use the money?" suggested Seymour. "Half a million dollars would buy you a new house and support you the rest of your life. You could even hire a nurse or someone to help with your grandfather. It would solve all of your problems."

"I hate that money more than I hate The House," spat Daniel. "How many people are dead because *Haverhill Chemicals* wouldn't release the vaccine? They made money while people were *dying*. Kids and parents. Fathers and . . ." he started to choke up. "I'll never touch that money."

"Then what will you do with it?" asked Dinora.

Daniel sighed. "I don't know but right now, I've got enough to worry about."

This sentiment was a somber cloud hanging over all of them and would have remained for the rest of the evening if other distracting events hadn't taken place.

After an hour or so had passed, the children heard a squeal from Dinora, who was standing at the large window.

"Everyone! Come quickly! Look at this!" she shouted.

The children rushed to join her. Fortunately, the immense library window afforded enough room for each of them to see what was about to play out on the lawn before them.

A shiny black Rolls Royce was approaching. It stopped in front of the house. Edith and Tia were just returning from their walk and Tia strode ahead to greet her visitor. All of this took place in silence, as the children were too far away to hear much, even though the windows were open to let in the summer breeze. As a result they could only suppose the true meanings of what followed.

A chauffer exited the car and opened the door for Mr. Billings. Tia welcomed him warmly and invited him inside. Although there was no obvious gesture indicating this, the children all agreed later it was safe to assume. Mr. Billings shook his head and Tia then motioned to the sitting area on the front lawn. He nodded and moved toward the intricately woven ironwork table, painted white with four matching chairs. He sat, as did Tia and then he stood and then sat again. He took off his Stetson and held it nervously in his hands. They seemed to speak for a minute and then, "Oh my!" Dinora exclaimed.

Mr. Billings knelt down on bended knee, withdrew a small black box from his jacket pocket, opened it and held it out so Tia could see.

"Tia, Tia, Tia. What have you been up to?" said Seymour, feigning shock.

"It's not as if she just sits around here all day, you know," said Zoë. "She has a life of her own."

"Apparently."

It was difficult to read the look on Tia's face because she turned and seemed to call for Edith. Her suitor turned also and rose to greet the approaching woman. He dusted off his knees and put the box into his left hand to shake Edith's with his right. Now Tia stood to join them, the three figures forming a triangle with Mr. Billings' back to the audience.

Tia spoke for a few minutes and as she did, Mr. Billings glanced repeatedly at Edith who stood there, occasionally nodding. When Tia finished speaking, Mr. Billings took Tia's hand and kissed it. He took Edith's hand, shook it, tipped his hat to both ladies and returned to his car.

"Ohhh," the children drawled in unison. After a long silence, Dinora said, "Now, *this* I've never seen on *Mis Secretos.*"

There was a chuckling sound and the children turned to see it was Dr. Sutton, smiling to himself.

Daniel beamed at Dinora. "He laughed!"

"Look! Mr. Billings is coming back!" she yelled, pointing to the driveway where another shiny black car was creeping toward them.

"That's not a Rolls, though," said Daniel.

The events they now watched were eerily similar to those from just a few minutes earlier. The chauffer stepped out and opened the door for a tall man to exit. It was the man from the courthouse.

"I'd take Mr. Billings over him any day," whispered Dinora.

"He's not here to propose, you ninny," said Zoë.

The man said a few words to Tia, who looked up to the library window.

"He's here to see me," stated Daniel.

"I'll stay with your grandfather, Daniel. You all go ahead."

"Thanks, Seymour. Grandfather, I'll be back in just a moment."

When Daniel exited the house, with his friends flanking him on either side, he made his way reluctantly toward the visitor.

"Mr. Sutton," the man addressed crisply, and somehow it didn't strike Greta as strange to speak to a fifteen-year-old in this way—especially Daniel.

Daniel didn't say anything.

"Sir, may we speak in private for a moment?"

Daniel seemed to consider this only briefly. "Anything you want to tell me can be said in front of my friends."

The man scanned the others. "Very well," he acquiesced disdainfully. "Sir, I've come on behalf of my client, who has arranged to provide you with some financial resources."

"Around here we just call that 'money'," said Zoë.

The man glanced sharply at the insolent girl and cleared his throat. "Yes, well. It is a *substantial* amount of financial security."

"How much?" Dinora asked excitedly.

"It doesn't matter," said Daniel acidly. "I don't want it."

"Well over twelve million dollars, U.S.," answered the man, as if he wielded sums of this magnitude on a daily basis.

"Wow," said Dinora. "That's security all right."

"And why doesn't your *client* just tell me all this himself?" demanded Daniel, motioning toward the car.

"I'm not at liberty to discuss that, sir."

"And why is he giving me so much money?"

The man cleared his throat again. "He wants very much to . . . help, sir." This emotional sentiment seemed more difficult for him to articulate.

"If you're not telling me where it's from, or why you're giving it to me, then I'm not taking it."

"Very well, sir, but I must inform you that my client instructed me to relay to you that if you refused, the funds would be deposited in the *Belfast Savings & Loan* under your name. If you should ever change your mind, it will be there for you. Good day, sir." The man returned to the car and the chauffer opened the back door. Another figure could be detected but not quite seen through the shadows and thickly-tinted windows. The children had no doubt who it was.

When the car was gone, Daniel sat down on the front steps and used both hands to support his head. "Oh great," he said. "More blood money."

The others didn't try to convince him otherwise. They knew it was useless.

27

❧ The Flowers ❧

Eli Eaton stood back to survey his handiwork. It wasn't the best porch he'd ever fixed, and it certainly didn't come close to the quality work Mr. Sands was doing on the roof, but it was passable and that was what mattered. They'd been working for six weeks—Tia's kids (that's what the locals called them) and an assortment of townsfolk. Gradually The House was resuming its former shape and character. They hadn't had time yet to work on the yard, which Mrs. Eaton had described as "an unholy mess" but Zoë had been clear in her instructions. Daniel and his grandfather needed a home. The garden could wait.

"Eli!" called Dinora. "Lunch is ready!"

Eli went into the renovated kitchen and washed his hands. Someone from church had donated a dining room table but the room was still floured in sheetrock dust so the workers preferred to eat on the lawn. Dinora had furnished enough blankets to convert the yard into what resembled a large park picnic. A door had been balanced between two sawhorses and Eli noticed that Dinora—or Greta, her constant companion—had draped it with a linen tablecloth. Delicious sandwiches were piled on one section, a large basket of fruit on another and a pitcher of lemonade in the middle.

The workers ate in contented silence, which gradually shifted into low murmurings of plans on what to do next. After reviewing their many accomplishments, they agreed the structural work was nearly complete. All that remained now was an incredible amount of cleaning.

"We can handle that," Seymour told them. "You've already done more than we ever expected. Thank you."

Edith returned from the final dump-run. Virtually everything from The House was ruined by water and had been thrown out. Seymour had scoured all the walls with his bleach solution until his eyes and hands were red. Finally, the stench of mold was gone. All of the windows had been kept open the entire time with the hopes that the cross breezes would help air out the rotted time capsule. A few things—dishes mostly—were salvageable. Other than those, the entire contents of The House were new. All of the walls had been painted white. The floors had been sanded, re-stained and glossed. Most importantly, there was a brand new roof.

This most expensive item was Eli's doing. He'd convinced the Ladies Aid Society to donate the extra funds from their highly-successful Monte Carlo Night. Now the church would get its new steeple and the Sutton House would be well-capped once again.

Buoyed by their tremendous success with The Steeple Fund, the L.A.S. had gladly spearheaded the refurbishing project. With Mrs. Emily Eaton setting a formidable and persuasive example, the determined women charged forth. Through soliciting and cajoling various shops and boutiques, they had produced quite a nice assortment of furniture and other sundries for The House. One of their many procurements was an armchair with remarkable similarities to the one now sitting in the *Deer Isle Dump*. The children couldn't agree if this would make it harder or easier for Daniel to accept The House as a home.

The Flowers

"Do you think he'll like it?" Dinora asked the others.

"I don't know," said Seymour. "It could be we've done all this work for nothing."

"He could always sell The House and live off the money," suggested Greta.

"No one's going to buy this house," Zoë scoffed. "No matter how good it looks. Even if he was innocent, it won't matter. Everyone will still think of it as The House."

As the children and workers packed up for the night and gradually made their way home, they were pleased with all they had achieved. In fact, the only person who wasn't pleased was the neighbor, Miss Fanny Pang, who spent most of the six weeks screaming out her window, either with her opinion that they were doing everything wrong, or with threats to call the authorities because they were creating a nuisance and scaring her bird. The threats ended when she discovered that Sheriff Phillips was heading up the sheet-rocking crew.

Finally it was done and the only thing left was to re-introduce The House to its owner. The children asked Tia to stay with Dr. Sutton and Edith agreed to drive them all over. Dinora blindfolded Daniel for his "surprise".

"What's all this about?" he asked nervously.

"You'll see, Danny," said Dinora coyly, barely able to contain her excitement. "A great big wonderful surprising surprise that will . . . surprise you!"

The drive took nearly half an hour and fortunately Edith had taken them in the *Ford Fairlane*. It was significantly more comfortable than the bed of an old Chevy pick-up.

They had decided earlier to remove Daniel's blindfold once he was directly in front of The House. They hadn't had the time to do anything about the garden and they didn't want its shabby state to further color his perception of the place.

"Are you ready?" piped Dinora.

"I guess," he said.

She untied the bandana and they held their breaths to see his reaction.

For a long time he said nothing—simply stared at The House, taking it all in.

Finally Dinora couldn't contain herself any longer. "I know you said you hated it but we thought if we fixed it up then maybe you'd reconsider. And we did! The whole town helped—well practically the whole town. It has a new roof and new walls and the holes are all fixed and it's not dangerous and there's furniture and Seymour got rid of the mold smell and I know your mom died in there and that your grandfather murdered someone except that he didn't and that The House made you throw up that day but, but, Danny, it *is* your house. It's—"

"I love it," he said matter-of-factly.

"You do?"

He nodded, turning to see all of them. There were tears in his eyes, which of course made the rest of them all start crying themselves. After enough tears, gratitude and congratulating, Daniel asked, "May I look inside?"

Mornings at Tia's were different now that Daniel was gone. It wasn't that they were any quieter, as the boy had rarely contributed more than a few sentences to the boisterous rumblings of the other children. It was simply that they knew he was gone.

"But we can go see him!" cried Dinora. "Shall we?"

"He doesn't have a phone so we'd have to just show up. Maybe he doesn't want company," said Greta.

The children had told Daniel to get a phone, that Tia would loan him the money—or, better yet, he could spend some of the money sitting useless in the briefcase.

But Daniel insisted he would never touch the money again.

"I've got enough in my college account to last us the rest of the year. If my grandfather gets better, I can go back to school next September. I'm not worried about that now. I just want to take care of him."

Upon hearing of Daniel's intention to drop out of high school, Tia nearly stormed over there herself to give her former charge a piece of her mind. The children barely managed to convince her to let him be. It had been a week ago, that they had helped Daniel and his grandfather move in and Dinora couldn't imagine why anyone would need more time than that "to themselves".

"Who wouldn't want company? I say we take the horses, race across The Island and see Danny. Oh! I just had a brilliant idea," she announced. "We could start working on the garden. I'm sure he hasn't had the time to do it himself and it's probably driving him crazy!"

"I'm sure he hasn't thought about it once and that *you'd* drive him crazy," muttered Zoë.

"Be nice," cautioned Seymour, who was beginning to detect Zoë's mean streak returning as they neared the end of summer. "I agree with Dinora. We told him to get a phone. He wouldn't, so he'll have to pay the price: unannounced company. To the barn!"

Normally, it would have taken fifteen minutes to be off and running but Tia insisted they bring lunch and Seymour remembered they'd need gardening supplies, so by the time they rode to the stream, crossed the recently-repaired bridge and knocked on the side door of the new and improved Sutton House, it was time for—

"Lunch!" Dinora greeted her friend.

They were all eager to see what Daniel had done with the place and were more than a little disappointed to see it looked pretty much the same as when they had left it.

"Danny, you need to make it your own," urged Dinora. "Do you want us to help?"

"You can't help someone make it their own," growled Zoë.

"I'm fine, Dinora. I love The House. I'm just a little preoccupied, that's all."

"Daniel, what's your grandfather doing?" asked Greta.

They all turned to look out the kitchen window, which faced the front lawn. The old man was wandering aimlessly.

"He looks like he's lost," commented Dinora. "Should we call him?"

Daniel laughed. "No. He knows I'm here."

"How's he doing?" asked Seymour earnestly.

"We've got good days and bad. Today's a good day. He remembers my name." Daniel smiled wryly.

"You're sure he's okay out there like that?"

"I'm sure. That's how he spends most of his day. He wanders around the yard, comes inside for a cup of tea and wanders around again and so on. Last night I woke up and couldn't find him. It was two in the morning and he's outside standing in the middle of that crazy lawn."

"Speaking of which," began Seymour, holding up a bag of gardening supplies, "we've come to help."

Daniel's expression revealed both his pleasure and relief. "Are you sure? It'll be quite an undertaking. Don't get me wrong. I'd love the help. I'm hoping to clear all this out and plant a garden. Then if Tia says it's okay, I'll continue the stall at the farmers market. I figure it will at least bring in a little income and I can keep Grandfather with me."

"Danny, that's a splendid idea. Of course Tia will let you. She'd like to do more but you're too stubborn. It kind of reminds me of this episode of *Mis Secretos* when Augusto is too prideful to accept help from his brother, Alberto, because of an unexplained family feud." Dinora looked at Greta. "They'll probably explain it in a future episode and I can write you all about it. So Augusto is about to lose everything until Alberto finds a way to give him money without his knowing about it." Dinora sighed deeply. "In the end, Danny, it just makes a mess of things."

"I'll keep that in mind, Dinora," said Daniel, trying not to laugh.

"Oh good, well then, I won't worry about it. What can I do to help?"

After convincing Daniel's grandfather to come in for lunch, the children chatted and ate—delighted to once again be in each other's company. After the meal was eaten and assignments given, they charged forth.

"Eep!" Dinora screeched as she ran right into a bizarrely-dressed old woman ascending the porch.

"Good heavens, you little demon! Watch where you're going!" scolded the woman, before turning to Daniel accusingly. "So you're back? Wonderful, just wonderful. Well, you listen here, pipsqueak—"

"Look at her shoes," Zoë whispered in Greta's ear.

Greta looked at the berating woman's feet. She wore gigantic shoes. Gigantic. "They look like clown shoes," said Greta.

"And so what if they are?" screeched the woman, whom all the children except for Daniel now recognized as the dreaded neighbor, Miss Fanny Pang.

"Sorry," mumbled Greta.

"I was the first female clown in a major circus. The first, missy. You hear that?"

"Yes, ma'am."

"Well, let's hope so. I was the first and I wear these shoes with pride. With pride I tell you, that I wear these shoes with pride in them."

"Ma'am, is there something I can—" Daniel began politely.

"Your old coot is scaring my bird!" she squawked.

"Pardon me?"

"Up and down and all around. All hours of the day, all hours of the night. How's an old woman supposed to get any sleep with all that ruckus?"

"My grandfather?"

"*My grandfather*," mimicked Miss Pang in a whiny voice. "Yes, your grandfather. I told him not to plant Gaillardia in the summer and you certainly don't plant it in the middle of the night. I'm glad they threw him in jail! Anyone who plants Gaillardia at night should go to jail. It's not Christian!" With this, Miss Pang and her enormous clown shoes stormed off—flipping and flopping—across the lawn.

The children looked at each other and shrugged—each at a loss for words.

Finally, Dinora said, "We should probably make hay while the sun shines."

"Okay troops, let's get to work!" ordered Seymour.

Greta and Dinora began working in the northwest corner of the sprawling lawn.

"Dinora, what do you make of this yard?"

Her companion surveyed the motley plantings and overgrowth. "It's something all right. Clearly Dr. Sutton wasn't much of a gardener. I barely know where to begin. We can't just leave it for Danny though. He's got enough on his plate."

"Doesn't it seem strange that he wasn't more of a gardener? Remember, in his yearbook, wasn't 'gardening' one of his hobbies?"

"Was it?" Dinora tilted her head. "I don't remember."

"And what you said too, about scientists being very organized—"

"I agree with that." She nodded emphatically.

"I don't know," said Greta. "Probably it's noth—"

Greta froze—a look of horror on her face.

"Greta? What's wrong?"

"Everyone, stop!" she screamed, running toward The House. "Dinora, make everyone stop!"

The others looked nonplussed but threw down their rakes and hoes and other garden implements and followed her into the house.

"Where'd she go?" Daniel asked the others, looking around the main floor.

"I'm up here!" came a voice from above them.

They stormed upstairs. "Where?" Daniel called.

"Up!"

"The attic?" asked Seymour.

"Must be," said Zoë. "Unless she's on the roof."

They bounded into the master bedroom, which included a closet and the narrow stairs to the attic.

"It smells so new up here!" said Dinora.

"What's going on?" asked Daniel, leading the others to meet Greta, who was standing next to the large window overlooking the lawn.

"Look at your grandfather," she instructed.

"He's walking," said Daniel flatly.

"No. All of you, come see. Look more closely."

They stared out the window for a while.

"What are we supposed to be seeing?" Dinora asked in a hushed whisper.

"Just wait a little longer. See where he's walking."

"He's just crisscrossing the lawn," said Daniel, irritation creeping into his voice.

"He's not, Daniel. Watch him. Don't think, just watch."

They continued to stare until Daniel threw up his hands in frustration. "Just tell me what I'm supposed to see, Greta. I don't get it."

"Sorry. I'm not trying to frustrate you. I wanted some confirmation, that's all. In case I was wrong. I didn't want to influence you. Never mind. Okay, right now, he's about to start again. This time I'll talk you through it."

They gazed down two stories below them, at the man who stood among a blaze of red daisies, their petals tipped with gold. He stayed there as if he wasn't sure what to do.

"What's happening?" asked Seymour. "Why's he just standing there?"

Greta shushed him. "He always does that. It's the starting place. Remember in his diary, he talked about the project and how he got *dirty*? Keep that in mind when— okay, he's starting. See how he goes past all of those other flowers to the ones on the far end of the lawn?"

They saw him make his way toward a clump of forest green leaves with large misty-pink plumes, which the children knew on closer inspection were actually red and white.

"That is the second point. Zoë? Will you grab some paper and a pen? Do any of you know what the first flowers are called?"

No one did.

"Does anyone know what any of them are called?"

They looked guilty.

"Sorry," said Daniel. "I know vegetables."

Seymour spoke up. "I know those are lavender there and I think this is wisteria, here on The House. I couldn't say for certain though. Look, he's heading back this way."

The children stood in awe as, one by one, the seemingly-random plantings were visited by a partially-demented old scientist. Each time he paused for just a moment, turned and slowly hobbled toward another group. At the red daisies he stayed for nearly a minute. They watched him repeat his cycle three times, to make sure. The third time, they sent Daniel down to follow him and take a sample of each flower. When they had labeled them in order and double-checked, they relaxed.

"It's the formula," said Greta. "I'm sure of it."

"But what does it mean?" said Daniel. "We're looking for chemicals—elements, not flowers."

"I have a theory on that too but I'll need a library."

"The one in town is closed by now. We'll have to go tomorrow," said Seymour.

"Not necessarily," smiled Greta. "I did a little organizing while I was going through Tia's books. I think her library has just what we need."

Daniel hated to let the others investigate without him. Seymour had offered to trade places but Daniel couldn't bring himself to leave his grandfather.

"We'll figure it out, Danny," promised Dinora. "Greta's great at stuff like this." She thumped the girl soundly on the back. "*¡Hasta mañana!*"

28

❧ The Formula ❧

The four children were seated at one end of the large mahogany table in Tia's library. There was an assortment of gardening and horticultural books opened, along with an antique copy of the Periodic Table. Other than four sets of elbows, the only other thing on the table was a bouquet of flowers, and that was not for decoration.

"So the red daisies with the yellow edges are called Dwarf Blankets, but Dr. Sutton was a botanist. He would have used their official name—their Latin name," instructed Greta.

"Then it's the Gaillardia," said Zoë, confirming this for the third time with the book in front of her.

"Right. And Gaillardia starts with 'Ga' which is the symbol for the element Gallium," announced Greta.

"I'm impressed, Greta," said Seymour.

"Wow," gaped an awestruck Dinora.

"Let's do the next one," ordered Zoë.

They each grabbed another flower, found its match in a botany book and then tried to find the coinciding element.

"Wisteria, wisteria," repeated Zoë. "'W!' That's Tungsten." She noted it on the label.

"Tungsten," laughed Dinora. "Tungsten. It sounds so silly. Tungsten."

"I've got another one," said Seymour. "The Clematis. That starts with 'Cl' which is the symbol for Chlorine. This is crazy! All this time, the world has been waiting for a vaccine that has been hidden in a bizarre garden. It's sad we didn't find it sooner," said Seymour.

Three hours later, they had nearly finished.

Dinora was done first and was trying to keep herself amused while she waited for the others. She turned her attention to the box of evidence they had collected. She picked up the small silver rattle.

"Do you mind?" said Zoë.

"Hmm?" Dinora asked, then realized she had been using the rattle to beat out a rhythm on the table. "Sorry."

"Hmph."

"Are you almost done?" asked Dinora.

"If I can *concentrate*, then I can *finish*. Stop that!"

"Oh, whoops." Dinora set aside the rattle. Less than a minute later, it had again found its way into her hands, being knocked repeatedly on the wooden table in a catchy beat.

"Give me that!" yelled Zoë, wrenching the rattle away.

The handle stayed in Dinora's grip and the top transferred to Zoë's. The contents, however, spilled out over the vast wooden floor.

"Oops," blurted Dinora.

Zoë made to get up, glowering at the younger girl.

"It's okay. I'll get them. It'll give me something to do," said Dinora cheerfully.

She began picking up the tiny silver beads, talking to herself. "One, two . . . there's another. Oh, no it isn't. I was wrong. I wonder how many were in there. Look, it's all scratched up inside. Hmm. *I'll be wearing ribbons down my back, this sum-merrrrrr.*" This last bit was sung quietly. It was her favorite song from *Hello Dolly!* and she had taken to singing it incessantly. And although she hadn't learned many of the lyrics, she had really aced that first line. "*I'll be wearing ribbons down my back, this sum-merrrr.*"

"Aargh!" Zoë screamed, scooting violently back in her heavy chair, which toppled over with a loud bang.

"Eep!" Dinora squeaked and then promptly laughed at the sound effect.

"Dinora, I just don't understand you! You're so stupid and silly. Not everything is a game. Not everything is fun. Not everything is happy! Sometimes life is miserable. But, no, Dinora's happy no matter what. Why, Dinora? What's there to be so happy about? Huh? Life isn't always good. Things don't always work out. What is it with you?"

Dinora looked at Zoë quizzically. "Life is good, Zoë," she said sweetly. "It's beautiful."

"Aargh!" Zoë howled with a rage none of the others had ever heard. Even Seymour. She was immediately consumed by tears and flew out of the room.

Seymour ran after her but she was faster and he didn't catch up until they reached the orchard. "Zoë!" he yelled.

The girl stopped and turned, still weeping uncontrollably.

Seymour approached. "What in the world is going on with you?"

"She drives me crazy!" Zoë blurted between sobs.

"Dinora's always like that. It's who she is. *You're* the one who's different. This whole summer you've been sullen and mean. *Mean*, Zoë. You've never been mean before. Why are—"

"I can't come back!" she screamed.

Seymour stood, stunned. "What do you mean?"

"I mean I—can't—come—back." Zoë tried to catch her breath. "*Nai Nai* made me swear. That's the only way they let me stay this year. I had to promise it would be my *last* summer. Seymour, I hate her. She ruins everything. She—" Zoë's words were lost in ragged crying.

Seymour went to his cousin, wrapping his arms around her. His head was flooded with memories from the past two months. Now it all made sense. *She's known this whole time*, he thought. His own heart ached as he imagined her keeping this to herself, week after week. He remembered the cruel things he had said to her. Sure, they were in defense of Dinora who, for some reason, bore the brunt of Zoë's pain and frustration, but he should have sensed something was wrong. He still couldn't believe *Nai Nai* would do that. *Well, what would I have done if my grandchild ran away and left the country?* he thought. *She must have been terrified, worried sick. A year from now things were sure to be different though.*

"Zo, *Nai Nai* will change her mind. Once she calms down." He relaxed his embrace to look her in the eyes.

Zoë sniffed, wiped her tear-stained face with her sleeve and looked at him. "She won't. I know she won't."

"I'm sure your parents—"

"They were the ones! It was *their* idea. They were furious when I ran away. They said it was an insult to *Nai Nai*, scaring her like that. They said they won't tolerate that kind of behavior. They made me promise this would be the last summer." She lost her battle with tears again and cried until her eyes were red and swollen.

Seymour held her again, fighting back his own tears. When her weeping had simmered she pulled away. "Seymour, they made *Tia* promise."

It was a few moments before Seymour responded incredulously, "And did she?"

Zoë nodded.

"Danny!" hollered Dinora, running through the excavated lawn to him. Breathless, she said, "You have mail." She panted a few more times, clutching her chest, before passing him two long white envelopes.

He took off his garden gloves and used his handkerchief to wipe the sweat from his brow.

"Let's read them inside," he said. "I could use a break and we should see how the others are coming along."

Upon entering the kitchen, Daniel set the envelopes on the counter and went to the sink to wash up.

"What's that?" asked Seymour. He and the others were circling the kitchen table in a vain attempt to piece together the formula."

"My first mail delivery. Any luck?"

"Sorry," said Greta. "We've tried everything. It's like cooking," she explained. "We have the ingredients and the order but we're missing the measurements and the process."

"Maybe we could give it all to someone who could figure the rest out," suggested Daniel.

"We could," said Seymour. "It might be our best option. Even so, it could take another scientist forever to finish someone else's work."

Daniel joined them at the table and opened the first envelope. He scanned it quickly, before muttering, "Great. This is the last thing I need."

"What is it?" asked Dinora.

"It's a bank statement from the account Lionel Robson set up for me. Apparently the interest this month is," he paused to read directly from the paper. "Seven thousand, four hundred and three dollars and sixty-three cents."

"Maybe you could just use a little of it, Danny. You'll run out of money soon," said Dinora.

"I know, I know. I can't. If I use one penny of it, I might as well use all of it. That's like me saying, it's okay to steal as long as I don't steal too much. I'd be a hypocrite," he argued. "Plus, if I take a little, I'm afraid I won't be able to stop."

"So what are you going to do with it?" asked Seymour.

"I don't know." He set aside the statement and reached for the second envelope. "It's from Lionel Robson," he said, showing the handwriting to the others before opening the letter. He read it first to himself, then aloud.

Daniel,

I can only imagine what you must think of me. I know an apology doesn't mean much but I am sorry. Truly, I am. When I left ten years ago, I never wanted it to end up like this.

Your feelings about the money are misdirected. I'm the one to blame. The money is merely money. You might as well use it. If it can bring the two of you some comfort, you should not let my mistakes stand in the way.

However, since my apology is worthless and you are too stubborn to accept the money, I will offer this last thing. I hope knowing the truth will bring you some solace.

Over ten years ago, your grandfather and I developed a vaccine for the influenza. As I'm sure you've deduced by now, George Huntington tried to buy us off. Haverhill was making a lot of money off the medicines. It wasn't "financially prudent" for them to release a vaccine. I understood and was more than happy to take the bribe. I am ashamed of that decision. I know it doesn't matter to you and that it is all done now but still, I deeply regret what I did.

Your grandfather refused. He was furious I would even consider it. I knew they wouldn't pay me if he wasn't included and I knew he'd never agree. I forged his signature and told Huntington I'd persuaded him to see sense.

After I got the money, we went out to the movies. I had the picture taken with the clock and the paper. I made sure the owner knew that your grandfather was there.

You've probably figured everything out. I faked my own death and framed him for it. I just needed him out of the way for a few days. I left the box so someone could prove his innocence. Truly, I don't know how it happened that the box wasn't delivered. It was only recently, when I decided to make amends in person, that I learned the truth.

I also don't know why he didn't speak in his own defense. He had a fair chance of proving his innocence without the evidence I left. You'll have to ask him why he went to prison so acquiescently.

If you are like your grandfather, and from what I've been told, you are, this last piece of information may cause you to pity me. This is not why I'm sharing it. If, on the other hand, you are anything like me, it might please you to know that I'm dying. Perhaps this is my punishment for hurting you, for betraying my friend, for the deaths of thousands. I don't know.

Daniel, I wish I could give you the formula. All my notes are gone and my memory is hardly reliable these days. Please take the money.

L.R.

"I was hoping he'd have the formula," said Daniel dejectedly. "Not that it would have made up for anything but at least—"

"Danny, I have an idea," said Dinora excitedly. "It's from *Mis Secretos* and the best part is I've seen it work."

Armed with a mission, Daniel marched to the headquarters of *Haverhill Chemicals*. He blew through the front door, past the addled receptionist and up to the fourth floor. He didn't even bother knocking on the polished door of Suite 400.

George Huntington emitted a startled sound. "Oh! Danny, so good to see you and what wonderful news about your grandfather," he said, quickly recovering his comportment. "Terribly sorry to hear he's not quite right in the—"

"Shut up," ordered Daniel coldly, glaring at him.

Dr. Huntington matched his gaze. "What manners, Danny," he said in his silkiest voice. "You should be careful of that. Members of civilized society might think those lovely nuns at *The Brewster Boys Home* didn't raise you properly."

Daniel's thinking veered off track. He considered this for a moment. "How did you know about the nuns?" he asked suspiciously. "You said you didn't know where I was. You said you'd lost contact with me," he accused.

Dr. Huntington rebounded easily. "So I lied. If you want to know the truth, *I'm* the one who took you there. Don't look so surprised, Danny. It's simply how the world works these days. A benevolent smile here, a little paperwork there and I had myself an assurance that Sutton would stay right where he was."

"You blackmailed him? With me—his own grandson?"

"I did what I needed to do." He chuckled to himself. "You should have seen the look on his face when he had to choose between your safety and his precious formula." Dr. Huntington's humor halted. "It was priceless," he said callously.

Daniel was flabbergasted, then furious. "How dare you?" he screamed, clenching his fists.

"It's just business, Danny. You understand business, don't you?"

"He was all I had. I was all *he* had. What kind of person—"

"A resourceful one." Dr. Huntington's voice hardened. "Listen, you have about thirty seconds before my security guards arrive, so if there's something you want to get off your chest, you should probably—"

"We've got it." Daniel fought his molten fury and forced himself to regain composure. If this was going to work, his anger needed to fuel him, not blind him.

His words caught Dr. Huntington's instant attention. "Got what?" he feigned disinterest.

"You know what, you miserable creep. You thought you could just let my grandfather rot in jail while you sat on it. What kind of man are you?"

"I'd say I'm a very content man, a very accomplished man. A very *rich* man."

"Oh, believe me, I know all about how much money you and your cronies made off this."

"You couldn't count that high, you little punk. And I wouldn't act so *holier-than-thou*. According to my sources, you've come into quite a tidy sum yourself, my boy."

"I am *not* your boy." Daniel got up to leave. "And I'm sick of you and this office so how about you listen to me this time? I've got the formula and I'm going to give it to *Proust Pharmaceuticals*. You may have heard of them. In fact, *my* sources say they're your number-one competitors."

"You're bluffing."

"Imagine the world hailing *Proust* as the savior of the human race—preventing thousands of deaths each year with their new wonder-vaccine. They might even win a Nobel Prize. Now I may not be able to count very high but I'm pretty sure something like that would prove quite lucrative."

"Don't mess with the big boys, Danny," Dr. Huntington sneered. "You might get into something you can't handle."

"I don't care what you do to me. You've robbed me of my family. What more can you do?"

"Use your imagination," said Dr. Huntington.

"Even if you do, I'm not the only one who knows."

"Children," he scoffed.

"They have mouths too and you can be sure they all know how to use a telephone. Look, you've had a good run of it, made a mountain of money for yourself and all your fat-cat friends, killed millions of people and now, the jig is up, you piece of filth." Daniel stormed out, slamming the door behind him and running down the four flights of stairs. And just in case Dr. Huntington was watching, Daniel made himself strut at a confident pace until he was out of sight.

Then he vomited.

Dinora and Daniel sat on the front porch of his house drinking hot chocolate. The evening had gotten cool and the others were inside discussing which card game they'd play. The only delay was that Dr. Sutton was still out in the garden. Rather than disturb him, Daniel preferred to wait until his grandfather was ready to come in for the night. Dinora offered a hot beverage and her company.

"When do you think we'll hear?" she asked.

"I don't even know if it worked," sighed Daniel. "And if it did, it could still be weeks or even months. I don't know how long it takes to do that kind of thing. Guess we'll just have to wait."

"Waiting is difficult."

Daniel smiled. "You know, Dinora. I have you to thank for all of it. When I realized we'd need more than the chemicals *included* in the formula to actually *make* the vaccine, I thought that was it—that we'd never have a chance. If you hadn't shared that story from *Mis Secretos* with us, I never would have imagined trying to trick people like *Haverhill Chemicals* into releasing it."

"I think it's the other way around actually," said Dinora intently. "I think the writers get their ideas from us. I think truth is stronger than fiction."

"You mean *stranger*?"

"That too," she replied, smiling.

ィ

❧ Epilogue❦

Bangor Daily News
Influenza Vaccine Near

Lifesaving news today for the millions of people around the world fighting the influenza pandemic. Haverhill Chemicals, the renowned pharmaceutical company, announced yesterday it is soon to complete the last of the clinical trials on a vaccine, to be possibly ready for the public by January.

"We're pushing hard," said Dr. George Huntington, "but we need to proceed with caution. These things take time and we want to do them right." Huntington is the Vice President of Haverhill Chemicals and heads up their research and development department. It was he who led the team that discovered the vaccine.

"There are a few defining moments in one's lifetime and this one is enough for ten lifetimes," Huntington said. "I'm honored that

Haverhill Chemicals is, once again, paving the way for a safer and healthier world." When asked about the rumors of a possible Nobel Prize, a humble Dr. Huntington replied, "We're not in the business of prizes. We're here to save lives."

2 September, 1969

Hello Danny!

It's been four days since we've been gone and I still miss The Island. Did you receive my other two letters? I know you must be bored with just your grandfather for company and he probably is still out in the yard so I thought I'd give you some interesting updates on my life in the past day.

Dulce María says that Maestra Reyna will be teaching history this year which is wonderful news. She is so old that she always forgets to give us homework. The other nice thing is that because she is so old, she's had a lot of interesting experiences. The other students say she tells great stories. Does that mean her memory is selective? Is your grandfather's memory selective?

I told Mario all about Horrible Haverhill. That's what I call them in my head. He said he didn't plan on interning for them again.

I guess that's it.

Love, Dinora

Epilogue

P.S. I completely forgot to tell you what happened with the brothers on Mis Secretos. Strangely enough, the situation still hasn't been resolved and I've been gone all summer! It's sure to happen soon though and I'll write you all about it.

27 September, 1969

Dear Seymour,

I thought a lot about what you said—about giving the money away if I wasn't going to use it. I decided you were right. It was driving me mad—the idea of it just sitting there, growing. Anyway, I talked to the bank and they helped me close out the account and wire the money to the Red Cross. I asked my grandfather where he wanted it to go but he didn't seem to understand. In the end, I was so anxious to get rid of it that I couldn't wait for an answer. Also, I figured the Red Cross does the kind of work he was trying to do. It felt fitting that it went to them. The bank also arranged it as an anonymous donation. This is good because I'd hate for them to get excited about another one. I'm not sure I'll be in the circumstances to give money away for a while.

Here's a strange thing. When I was at the bank I asked them if my grandfather still had an account. I don't know what made me think of it. They checked and he did. It took some time to access it but once I did, there was plenty in there. Not like the other account, of course, but enough for us. It came just in time, since we owed ten years in back taxes! I never thought this is what my life would be like at fifteen but I'm grateful for it—for him—every moment.

Thank you for being such a good friend.
Daniel

4 October, 1969

Dear Greta,

I got good news today and I knew you would be the one person most excited about it. I'm going back to school. Well, sort of, anyway. In September, the school board said I couldn't do my work from home, but today I got a letter in the mail saying they had changed their minds. I thought it was pretty strange but then Tia dropped by this afternoon "just to say hello" and I figured she must have had something to do with it.

It will be a lot of work—to catch up on the month I missed but I met with the teacher and he was very nice. Grandfather is doing better every day. I don't want to get too ahead of myself, but if things keep going like this, I might be able to go back to school for real next semester.

It's late and I'm trying to catch up on some work before I go to sleep. We'll get up early tomorrow and head into town for market. Edith loaned me the truck until I can figure out something on my own. Grandfather comes with me and helps in the stall. After market we'll go to Doc and Mrs. Ingraham's for lunch and bridge. Grandfather enjoys seeing his old friends and it took no time at all to remember how to play. Just when I think he's confused, he'll bid and make a baby slam! Doc Ingraham says it is like that sometimes, with memory loss.

How are your languages coming?

Please write soon. It can get lonely sometimes.

Daniel

Epilogue

27 November, 1969

Dear Zoë,

Today is Thanksgiving. It's a little after eight in the morning and I'm trying to do my homework. Can you tell? Anyway, I still have four days and I've been meaning to write you for a while now. I hope things are going well with you. I know it's difficult but in a little over nine months you'll be back on The Island and we can plan a week-long trip on The Prudence. Maybe we can head up to Nova Scotia. Wherever we go, it's sure to be fun.

Speaking of fun, I ran into Eli Eaton the other day. He asked after you and told me to say "hello" for him. I'm just the messenger.

Zoë, this summer you seemed out of sorts. It took me awhile to notice because of everything that was going on with me but now that things are settling into a normal routine, I've had more time to reflect. I hope whatever it was that was worrying you has been resolved.

I'm sorry for yelling at you this summer. I wanted to tell you that. I know you'll understand and forgive me and say it's not a big deal, but it is to me. I don't have a lot of friends and for a long time you and the others and Edith and Tia were my only family. Family means everything to me. When you don't have any, you wish you did but after a while you just accept it and don't really think about it so much. When you have a family, it's hard to think of how you ever could have gotten on without one. Anyway, I wanted to apologize.

We'll be heading over to Tia's this afternoon for Thanksgiving dinner. I think the Eatons will also be there so I'll be sure to tell Eli you said "hello" back.

Grandfather is doing much better. He still has days where he's confused but more and more he's remembering things. I try not to get my hopes up but it's difficult not to imagine what life might be like a year from now. Today being Thanksgiving doesn't feel too different. Ever since we moved home I've been grateful for every moment. Still, something special happened last night and it seems right that it took place this weekend. After dinner, Grandfather told me a story about my mom.

I hope this is enough postage.

Your friend always,

Daniel

About the Author

Robin Russell teaches writing to fifth graders. *A Jail for Justice* is the second book in the *Summer Island* series. Ms. Russell lives with her family in Seattle, Washington. For more information, visit www.robinrussell.net.

LaVergne, TN USA
30 April 2010
181205LV00001B/1/P